TOM SWIFT™

young inventor

Don't Miss Tom's Next adventures!

TOM SWIFT™

young inventor

#1 **INTO THE ABYSS**

By Victor Appleton

Aladdin Paperbacks
New York London Toronto Sydney

ALADDIN PAPERBACKS
An imprint of Simon & Schuster Children's Publishing Division
1230 Avenue of the Americas, New York, NY 10020
copyright © 2006 by S&S Inc

Designed by Lisa Vega
The text of this book was set in Weiss.
Manufactured in the United States of America
First Aladdin Paperbacks edition June 2006
2 4 6 8 10 9 7 5 3 1

Library of Congress Control Number 2005935356
ISBN-13: 978-1-4169-1518-8
ISBN-10: 1-4169-1518-4

Contents

Midnight Mission

"Something tells me we shouldn't be doing this, Tom."

It was dark—pitch-black, except for my laser flashlight.

I pointed it at the steel door's lockbox, pulled out my coded key card, and prepared myself for action.

"Take it easy, Yo. Just trust me on this, okay?"

I don't normally call people "Yo." In this case, though, it fit perfectly. "Yo" is short for Yolanda—Yolanda Aponte, that is—one of my two best friends.

The other is Bud Barclay, who at the moment was standing right behind Yo, peeking over her shoulder at me.

"She's right, Tom," he said. "This place is closed for

the night. We've got no business being on the aquarium grounds, let alone inside the building!"

"Yeah," Yo said. "You think, just because your name is Swift, you have special privileges?"

"Actually, yes. Swift Enterprises is a big contributor to the Shopton Aquarium's fund-raising efforts. In this case, I called in advance and got special permission to visit after hours. See?" I smiled and held up my key card.

"Permission for *tonight*?" Bud asked. "Then how come nobody's here to meet us?"

"They said they'd send someone down to escort us," I admitted. "I don't know why they're not here on time, but now that we've dragged all this stuff down here, it would be a shame to lug it all back to the lab without trying it out."

I had a big metal suitcase with me, and Bud was carrying a large plastic cooler. It's hard to say which one was heavier.

"Besides, they gave me the key card, didn't they?"

"So?" Bud asked.

"So, I took that to mean it's okay for us to at least get started without them."

It was actually fine by me that they hadn't shown up on time. I preferred to try out my newest, hottest invention free from prying eyes.

I mean, you never know when someone might steal your great idea. Scientists are dedicated people, of course—but there are more than a few sharks in the water (*sharks in the water*—get it?).

The point is, ideas are more precious than gold and a lot easier to copy. Swift Enterprises—my dad's company, where I have my own lab—is on the cutting edge of the idea universe. So secrecy is always key—and tonight was no exception.

"You haven't even told us why we're here," Bud said, as I slid the key card into the slot. With a sharp click and a pneumatic sucking sound, the doors opened, and I stepped inside the darkened main lobby of the Shopton Aquarium.

"Come on in," I said to my friends. "Hurry up!"

"What, you mean before someone sees us?" Yo raised her eyebrows suspiciously but shuffled in anyway. "I feel like a criminal."

Bud was right behind her. "We'd better not get in trouble for this," he said, looking left and right.

"Guilty conscience?"

"Cut it out, Tom," he said. "I'm on the edge of bookin' right now."

"Bud, Yo, they said they'd be here, and I'm sure they'll show up eventually. Don't worry so much, okay? I have permission for us to be here. I promise you—I spoke directly with Dr. Harrod, the aquarium director."

They didn't look convinced. "Come on. Have I ever steered you guys wrong?"

They took way too long to answer that one—but then they both cracked up laughing, and I knew they were in. As usual, they were along for the ride, no matter where it took us.

I led them down the hallway, past darkened tanks full of exotic sea creatures, until we reached the door at the far end.

The sign overhead said, SHARK TANK: EMPLOYEES ONLY.

"I knew there was something *fishy* about this," Yo said, cracking a smile.

The door to the room was locked. I set down the metal suitcase I was carrying. Then I reached into my vest pocket and pulled out a sweet little electronic device I'd invented just a few months earlier. I was glad I'd thought to bring it along with me tonight.

"What's the matter?" Bud asked. "Key card won't work?"

I gave him an annoyed look. No, it wouldn't, as a matter of fact. I hadn't thought to ask Dr. Harrod if there was a separate code for the shark tank room.

I showed Bud and Yo what was in my hand. It looked like a tiny turtle with blinking red eyes and a digital readout on its shell.

"What in the world is that?" Bud said.

"Ooh, it's so cute!" Yo said, reaching over to pet it.

"Nah, nah, nah," I said, yanking it away from her. "Don't touch. It's very sensitive."

"But what is it?" Bud questioned, his hands on his hips.

"I'm glad you asked," I said, throwing an arm around his shoulder. "It's a Tom Swift Jr. original—my brand-new electronic key code reader."

"Wow," Yo said, still in love with the cute little electronic turtle. "That's so cool! How does it work?"

"Watch this," I said. I held the turtle to the side of the door, where the lock slot stuck out an inch or so. Then I slipped my key card in and back out of the slot.

The red light on the lock box lit up, signaling that the code on my key card didn't match the correct one.

Ah, but my handy-dandy turtle mini–code-reader had locked onto the chip inside the lockbox, and it had read the correct code as it was compared to my card's incorrect one!

Now all I had to do was touch the little wonder-gizmo to my own card, and its magnetized code would change to match.

"Ta-da!" I said, as the doors to the shark chamber slid open for us. "Open, sesame!"

"You are such a show-off," Bud said.

We all went inside the shark room. Before we realized what was happening, the heavy metal doors swung shut behind us, plunging us into sudden darkness.

"Oh, great," Bud said. "Now what?"

"No worries," I said, fishing out my laser flashlight. Shining it around the room, I soon found the circuit-breaker box and turned on the juice.

Ten thousand watts of light flashed on at once.

To avoid being blinded, we had to cover our eyes until they had time to adjust. Then, we looked around the enormous chamber, with its huge circular tank of water at its center.

"There's got to be a dimmer box," I said, still shielding my eyes. I found it and turned the lighting down to a normal level.

I could see now that the water in the tank glowed green, lit from underneath. Dark, sinister shadows circled beneath its calm surface.

Now, the Shopton Aquarium isn't one of the world's biggest. Coney Island Aquarium, in Brooklyn, is the state's premier facility—and there are a few others that have ours beat in most categories.

But as far as sharks go, Shopton is number one.

The tank is forty feet across and thirty feet deep, and it has more varieties of shark mixed together than you'd ever find in nature, or in any of those other aquariums I mentioned.

To get in on the action visitors have to walk down a wide spiral staircase to the tank's two lower levels. There, they can see the sharks through the thick, plate-glass walls of the tank. It's well worth a visit—especially at feeding time.

That's when the keepers throw fish in the water, and the sharks suddenly come to life. In two seconds they go from swimming slow, lazy circles in the tank to darting from side to side, snatching and grabbing at the food.

Soon, there's nothing left but a huge cloud of tiny fish pieces. Tiny flakes float slowly down and are eaten by the smaller sea creatures living in the sand and rocks that line the tank's bottom.

At the end of the demonstration, for a spectacular grand finale, the keepers throw in raw steaks. The blood filters into the water. You can see it—trails of red, like smoke wafting through the water.

Sharks have extremely sensitive noses. They can smell the scent of blood from great distances—some shark species can detect a drop of blood from a mile away. In the confines of the shark tank, the smell of blood drives them into a feeding frenzy.

In this condition, the sharks are truly frightening. Everyone watching thanks their lucky stars for the thick glass wall between them and all those razor-sharp teeth.

Only, in my case, there wasn't going to be any glass wall. There would be nothing at all, except for my pressure-proof diving suit—and my other incredible new invention—the Swift Kick Shark Zapper.

Bud was leaning over the railing of the tank, peeking down at the circling sharks. "This is creeping me out," he said.

"I wouldn't lean over the tank like that," I said. "One of them might take a bite out of you."

"Whoa!" Bud leaned back in a hurry and stumbled away from the railing.

"I was just messing with you," I said, laughing.

Sharks don't usually leap out of the water to snatch a meal, but Bud apparently didn't know that. Strange—he knows just about everything else.

See, Bud's a genius—he knows more facts about more subjects than anyone I've ever met—but nobody ever mistook him for a daredevil.

"Hey." I put a hand on his shoulder. "You're gonna have a great scoop for the *Shopton Gazette*, so just hang with me here, okay?"

"Okay." He blew out a breath of air, trying to calm down.

Bud writes for our school paper—in fact, he wants to be a writer someday. He's good, too.

Of course, a lot of his stories are about his adventures with me and Yo. We've been in a lot of extreme situations together. Assuming everyone survives those kinds of things, they make for pretty interesting reading.

"Enough suspense, Tom. What are we here for?"

Yo's hands were planted on her hips, and she was standing right next to my metal suitcase. Inside was my newest invention—the one we were here to try out.

"I was just about to tell you," I said. "I would have mentioned it before, but . . ."

"But you were afraid we'd back out," Bud said, finishing the sentence for me.

"Well . . ." I shrugged. "Anyway, let me show you this baby."

I crouched down and placed my fingertip on the suitcase's identifier pad. A line of green light moved across its surface from below, scanning my fingerprint. A second later, the case unlocked itself. I opened it.

"Whoa!" Bud said. "What is *that*?"

I could tell Yo was impressed, too, though she didn't say a word.

"It's a deep-sea diving suit," I said.

"Yeah, we can see that," Bud said. "But what's it made of?"

The shimmering blue-green metallic material of the suit was unique—patented and secret. "It's a carbon-based composite," I said. "I developed it based on the molecular structure of snakeskin. Um, this is just between us, okay?"

They both nodded. "Of course," Yo said. "Go on."

"Snakeskin is incredibly strong, lightweight and flexible—also, carbon-based. With the help of our array of electron microscopes, I reconfigured the carbon molecules, then grew them in a special medium and combined the end-product with Swiftglass—well, it gets a little complicated from there."

"*Gets* a little complicated?" Bud said. "I'm already lost."

Genius or not, Bud sometimes has a tough time with the scientific stuff. I have to help him with his homework most of the time, but it's a fair exchange. All the classes where I'm clueless—history, geography, languages, social studies—well, like I said, he's a genius . . . just a very unscientific one.

"Anyway, the really cool part is that the suit—*in theory*, at least—should hold up under pressure as deep as fifteen thousand feet below the surface of the ocean. That would be a new record, by far."

"Awesome!" Yo said, fingering the material. "But what about breathing? I've been scuba diving, and when you get down deep, I know you can't stay down as long."

"Good question, Yo," I said. "Here's how."

I lifted out the suit's specially designed air-supply system. It consists of a tank containing, not compressed air, which wouldn't last you a minute down at fifteen thousand feet, but a unique mixture of oxygen, helium, and other additives.

"With this, plus a specially modified rebreather to recycle the gases," I said, "a full tank will buy you an hour and a half without refilling."

"Wow!" Yo said.

"That's a huge advance in deep-sea diving technology," Bud said. "But don't you get cold that far down? How do you keep from freezing?"

"Another good question. You stay warm because of a special argon-gas-filled layer between the inside and outside of the suit. It's super-charged to provide extra insulation."

"Cool," Bud said.

I smiled. "You mean warm. And not only could you get that far down, stay down for that long, *and* stay warm while you're at it, but because I embedded mechanical mercury servos—tiny motors implanted all over the suit that serve as boosters for your muscles—you should be able to move around pretty normally."

They looked at me blankly, so I went on explaining. "At fifteen thousand feet, you wouldn't be able even to move without the servos. Too much pressure."

"And without the suit?" Bud asked.

"You'd crumple like a piece of paper."

Yo gave me a piercing look. "Okay, but this shark tank here is only thirty feet deep. You didn't come here to test out how the suit handles deep-ocean pressure."

"Aha!" I said, smiling at her. "You're right, Yo. You're exactly correct. I brought the suit along for protection—because it's strong enough to stand up to a shark bite."

"*In theory*, at least," Bud said, throwing my own words right back at me.

"Couldn't you just put the diving suit on a crash dummy and send it down there to get chomped on?" Yo asked. "I mean, why do *you* have to be inside it?"

"Because there's something attached to the suit, Yo. Something that I need to try out."

"Something to do with sharks?" Bud guessed.

"Yup. It's my new ultra-sonic, super-duper Swift Kick Shark Zapper."

I showed them the control panel on the back of the diving suit's left glove. "I press here to activate it."

"What does it do? Give them an electric shock?" Yo asked.

"No—that wouldn't work too well. Water conducts electricity, remember? I would fry myself, along with all the sharks."

"Oh. Right." She giggled, her hand flying to her mouth. "I knew that."

"This zapper's actually kind of radical—if it works the way I think it will. . . ."

I was already putting the suit on, with a little help from my friends. The snakeskin-type material is form-fitting and clingy, and putting it on yourself can take awhile.

"How does it work, then?" Bud asked. "In English, please."

"When a shark comes in to attack, it instinctively closes its eyes—to protect them. With its eyes closed, the shark detects movement using a tiny sensor in its nose, which picks up the electromagnetic waves emitted by its prey."

"Now *that* is *cool*," Bud said. He reached for his notepad, about to write it all down—then stopped, remembering we were dealing with trade secrets.

"The actual zapper is embedded in the helmet of the suit," I said, lifting it up to show them. "It emits an electromagnetic pulse that's far stronger than what normally comes off a human being. In fact, the pulse is so strong, it overloads the shark's sensor, causing a painful sensation that drives the shark away."

"I'm surprised the aquarium gave you permission to try it out," Yo said. "Ever heard of animal cruelty?"

I waved her off. "It only stuns the shark for an instant. There's no lasting harm done—and if it works, Yo, think of all the lives it'll save! Divers, surfers, people wearing life preservers."

"I guess that's true," she said.

"And it could protect the sharks, too," I added. "Do you know how many sharks are caught by mistake by commercial fishing boats? So many that several shark species are going extinct! But if you put my Swift Kick Shark Zappers on all those miles-long fishing lines, they'll keep sharks from getting hooked by mistake!"

"*In theory*," Bud repeated. "Assuming it works."

"Well," I said, "that's what we're here to find out."

Reaching into the side compartment of the metal suitcase, I pulled out a wireless receiver/transmitter and handed it to Bud. "Here," I said. "So we can talk to each other while I'm down there."

"Okay," he said. "But what if there's a problem?"

"What problem could there possibly be? Even if the Zapper's a bust, the suit will protect me. If it'll fend off water pressure at fifteen thousand feet, it should be able to deal with the pressure of a shark's jaws."

I pointed to the cooler Bud had been carrying. "Open it," I said.

He did, and lifted out two clear, sealed plastic bags of bloody raw hamburger.

"I'll take one of those down with me," I said.

"What?! Are you nuts?" Yo screamed.

I turned back to Bud. "You keep the other bag," I told him. "In case I use mine up, you can drop it in the tank to keep the sharks excited."

Bud rolled his eyes. "You are one crazy dude," he said.

"Yo," I said, "I'm going to need your help locking

on this helmet. It's a little tricky with the gloves on."

"No!" she said, shaking her head violently. "I'm not gonna help you get yourself killed!"

"I'll be fine, Yo. Hey, you've helped me plenty of times before when it wasn't exactly safe."

"Nothing this dangerous."

"Oh really? What about that time at the volcano?"

"Um . . . well . . ."

"And that nuclear spill?"

"Okay, okay," she said. "I get your point. Just be really, really careful, okay?"

I patted her on the shoulder. "You know I always am."

2

Shark Food

I lowered the helmet onto my head, and Yo locked all the seals, making the entire suit airtight. "Testing, testing," I said. "Can you read me, Bud?"

His voice came through the helmet's communications system. "I read you loud and clear, Tom."

"Cool. Well—here goes nothing." I gave my friends the thumbs-up sign and climbed over the side of the tank.

Taking a deep breath, I let go of the railing, working the regulator so that I sank gradually to the bottom.

All around me, like slow-moving dancers, the sharks circled. There were smaller ones—the babies and juveniles called "dogfish"—as well as a couple dozen larger ones.

I'm no expert, but I could easily pick out several tiger sharks, a few makos, a pair of hammerheads with their weird rectangular heads, and to top it all off, an enormous, terrifying great white—the kind from the movie *Jaws*. You know—the one that eats the whole boat?

For the first time that night, I felt a shiver of fear go through me. I knew the sharks were checking me out, even if they didn't change course. Each of them was sending out electromagnetic pulses that bounced off the material of my shark suit, sending back signals about the strange, shimmering fish that had suddenly appeared in their midst.

See, sharks never really sleep. They have to keep moving in order to breathe—which they do by filtering oxygen from the water that passes through their gills. So to get some rest, they close one eye at a time and, presumably, rest half their brain as well.

But nothing wakes them up like a little blood in the water—and I had come here to wake them up.

I took a deep breath, hoping my little experiment went as planned, and unsealed the bag.

I watched as the trail of blood expanded like red smoke into the green water. I had a pretty good idea of what the sharks were about to do.

The dogfish got excited first, as little children will. They quickly moved in on me, trying without success to bite through my shark suit. I could feel them nibbling, but they couldn't get a good grip on the hard, slithery, flexible material.

It kind of tickled, to tell you the truth. I tried to hold still, though. I was waiting for the big ones to strike.

I sure hoped my Swift Kick Shark Zapper worked. My suit was designed to withstand incredible pressure, sure—but *evenly applied* pressure, like at fifteen thousand feet, not the *concentrated* pressure of a shark's teeth. If the suit got punctured, its strength would disappear in an instant. The sharks could chew right through it—and right through me, too!

One of the hammerheads flicked its tail. A fraction of a second later the entire tank exploded into chaos, as all the sharks went ballistic at once.

I screamed inside my helmet and hit the zapper button for all I was worth.

Wow!

There was no sound, but the circle around me

instantly expanded, as the sharks retreated to the glass walls of the tank.

"You okay down there, Tom?" Bud's voice crackled in my ear.

"Fine! The zapper works!"

"Congratulations, brother. Now come on up, okay?"

"Not yet," I told him. "I've got to see how long it keeps them away."

Sure enough, a minute or so later, they came at me again.

Once more, the zapper did its job. I breathed a huge sigh of relief, and smiled.

Not only was I still alive but it also looked like the Swift Kick was a winner.

And just then, wouldn't you know it, my suit's power shorted out.

First, the readout on the back of my left glove went dark. Then, I could hear the crackle of static as I lost voice contact with Bud.

Great. Just great. I now had no zapper, no contact with Bud—and I was surrounded by a tank full of sharks in the middle of a feeding frenzy!

I'm telling you, I felt like a total moron. Five minutes ago I'd assured Yo that I was always careful. Yet I hadn't even bothered to check and see if the suit's battery was fully charged.

Ooof!

I felt the air get knocked out of me as the first shark hit. Luckily it had only been a timid, half-hearted attack. Most of the sharks were still reeling from the zaps they'd gotten.

It would take them a few moments to get their courage back, but only a few. With all that blood in the water, nothing would hold them back for long.

I started removing the weights that had dropped me down to the bottom. But it was hard to bend over in the diving suit, and I kept getting body-slammed as the big sharks started coming in for the kill.

I had to get all the weights off before one of them clamped its jaws down on—

YEEOOOWWW!!

Just as the thought crossed my mind, a monster set of jaws chomped down on my midsection with incredible force.

It had to be the great white! It was tossing me around in its mouth like I was a little rag doll!

I thought I was going to pass out from sheer terror. I could hear my heart hammering in my ears, and I could feel the blood rushing to my head.

Luckily, the material of the suit didn't rupture. It resisted the shark's jaw pressure just enough so that my body didn't get totally squished.

Don't get the idea it was a picnic, though. I had no air left in my lungs, and with Jaws clamped down on my abdomen, no way was I taking another breath any time soon.

I was all out of solutions. If Bud and Yo had any ideas, now was the time to try them.

Suddenly, just as I was about to pass out, the jaws of death released me! I greedily sucked in a lungful of air from my suit's tank.

I wasted no time unhooking the remaining weights keeping me down. Then, without kicking around too much—I didn't want to attract any more attention—I let myself rise slowly toward the surface.

Now I could see why the great white had let go of me. At the far end of the tank, Bud was chucking meat from his baggie into the water!

Good old Bud to the rescue! The shower of bloody hamburger had drawn the whole crowd of hungry sharks its way.

I waved my arm to get Yo's attention. I wanted her

to come over to the railing and help drag me up and over.

Unfortunately, I also drew the attention of one of the sharks. It turned around and came right for me.

I threw up my left arm to protect myself, and the shark bit down on it hard. With my arm in its jaws, it dragged me back down toward the bottom of the tank.

The shark's teeth were embedded in the zapper's control pad on the back of my glove.

No! My fantastic invention, totally mangled!

I realized now that I'd made the control panel too vulnerable—a definite design flaw. I made a mental note to correct it, *if* I lived through this nightmare.

What an idiot I was! How had I gotten into this mess? I gave myself a smack in the forehead with my free hand—and amazingly, the zapper came back to life!

The shark let go of me and sped away as fast as it could go. I kicked hard, rising quickly to the surface. At the same time I made for the edge of the tank. As I got there, Yo leaned over, grabbed me, and hauled me over the side wall to safety.

"Tom! Are you okay?" she cried as she lifted the helmet off me.

I sank back onto the floor, exhausted but thrilled to be alive. "I've been better," I said. "My arm hurts, my stomach hurts—breathing hurts."

"I can't believe we let you go in there!" Bud said, glancing back at the tank. The water was still frothing, as the sharks fought over the last bits of steak.

"Hey," I said, "I owe you one. You guys saved my life."

Yo shrugged it off. "Like you haven't saved ours a dozen times."

I exhaled deeply. It hurt, bad. "I'm gonna have to . . . work out a few kinks."

"You're gonna have to take an X-ray," Bud corrected me.

"I meant the suit. . . ."

He laughed, shaking his head, then looked at Yo. "He'll live."

"Yup," Yo agreed. "Same old Tom Swift."

3

An Ocean Voyage

The next afternoon we were all over at Snyder's Ice Cream Parlor, chowing down on a Kitchen Sink Sundae (seven flavors of your choice, all the different toppings, enough for an army—their slogan should be "come hungry, leave bloated").

My arm was still sore where the shark had bitten down on it, even though I'd been icing it overnight and all that morning. I could tell that nothing was broken, but the bruises hurt plenty. My chest was killing me too where the great white had grabbed me. The dozens of purple tooth marks on my chest made it look like I'd gotten a shark bite tattoo.

"Well, Tom," Bud said as he glurped down a huge

scoop of chocolate heaven. "I'll bet you're glad that's all over with."

"Over with?" I lowered my spoonful of monster mint chip. "Who said it's over with?"

"Oh, no, come on," Yo said. "You're not dragging us back there again. No way!"

I smiled. "We're done at the aquarium," I promised. "The zapper worked fine, apart from the power. But I've got to work on the suit's design—especially the controls. And I might want to tweak it a little, to make it more puncture-proof."

"Good thought," said Bud. "Take your time fixing it, Tom. No rush. No rush at all."

"Actually, there *is* a rush, kind of." I leaned back in my chair and put my hands on my full stomach. "How would you guys feel about a little ocean voyage?"

"You mean like a cruise?" Yo asked, brightening. "I *love* cruises! My *abuela* took us on a cruise to Puerto Rico last year, and it was amazing! They had all kinds of entertainment. And the food? Fabulous!"

I shook my head. "This will be a little different. My dad's going out for a couple of days on a research vessel next week, and he invited us to come along."

"Oh." Yo seemed disappointed, but Bud was suddenly interested.

"You mean, like that Cousteau guy? Can we go down in one of those deep-sea submersibles and find all new species of fish?"

"Uh, no. Not *you* guys, anyway. You'd be staying on the ship with the researchers and scientists and crew."

"And *you*?" Yo asked me.

I crossed my fingers. "I'm hoping," I said.

They both knew what I meant. This was the perfect chance to test out my Swift Kick Shark Zapper *and* my deep-sea diving suit, under real world conditions.

"When is the ship sailing?" Bud asked.

"Next week, on Tuesday. I know it's kind of last-minute, but my dad only told me about it this morning."

"What makes you think they'd take me and Bud?" Yo asked. "I mean, we'd be pretty useless to them—just dead weight."

She looked over at Bud, who's not overweight—except that he'd just eaten about four scoops of ice cream, and his stomach was sticking up like a beached whale under his shirt.

Bud nodded toward the empty tureen that had

held the Kitchen Sink Sundae. "A whole *lot* of dead weight," he said.

"Really, Tom," Yo said. "Why would they agree to take us? We'd be worse than useless."

"No you wouldn't," I told her. "But I'm sure they could use your help on their computers, Yo—you're so great at that stuff. And Bud—well, there's a whale of a story there for the *Gazette*, right?"

They looked at me with raised eyebrows.

"Besides, you wouldn't be useless to *me*," I went on. "Have you forgotten already? You guys saved my life last night."

Yo blinked. "Oh. Yeah. We did, didn't we? Hah. I guess you're right—we'd better come with you to keep an eye on you and make sure you don't do anything stupid."

"That's the spirit," I said, patting her shoulder. "Besides, I already asked my dad if you could come, and he said yes." I turned to Bud. "You in?"

Bud didn't hesitate. "Hey, man," he said, "I can't swim that well, and I'm scared of sharks, not to mention drowning, but a chance to watch deep-sea exploration up close and personal? I wouldn't miss it—not for ten Kitchen Sinks."

○ ○ ○ ○

"How come *I* don't get to go with Dad on the ship?"

My sister Sandy was sitting across the breakfast table from me, holding her cereal spoon in her hand like she was going to start banging it on the table.

Sandy is a year younger than me, and she always has to do everything I get to do. She can be a real pain sometimes, but I'll tell you, there's no better basic research scientist at Swift Enterprises—or anywhere else, for that matter. Sandy is a huge brain, with a photographic memory on top of it, and sometimes, that makes her even more of a pain.

"I'm going because I have some new inventions I want to try out," I explained.

"Oh, yeah? Like what?"

I told her about the diving suit and the shark zapper.

"Those don't sound so great," she said, stirring the milk in her bowl in search of one last corn flake. "I think I should get to go this time."

"And what, try out your newest mathematical theorem?"

Sandy stamped her feet. "I *never* get to go anywhere or do anything cool!"

"Sandy," Mom said, coming into the kitchen,

"finish your breakfast and stop pestering your brother. You know you went with me to New York last spring for the international sculpture exhibition."

Mom is a well-known sculptor herself. She specializes in those huge prehistoric animals you see at museums of natural history.

Sandy made a face. She knew she had no argument. In New York she and Mom had gone to two Broadway shows, seen three real-live movie stars crossing the street, and bumped into two Nobel Prize–winning scientists in an elevator.

"Tom, you haven't eaten a thing," Mom said. "Aren't you hungry?"

"Not really. I'm actually kind of tired, to tell you the truth."

"Oh? Is something the matter?"

"No, I'm fine—I was just up most of the night, working on the diving suit's control panel," I said. "I still haven't gotten it quite right."

She leaned over and kissed me on the forehead. "Well, don't worry, you will. You always do in the end, when you put your mind to it."

"Hmph," Sandy grunted. "His calculations are probably off."

"Sandy," Mom said, "you know, I'm going to Washington this weekend for a show at the Smithsonian Institution. Would you like to come along?"

That got her. Sandy dropped her spoon right in the milk, sending a shower up that got her shirt—not that she even noticed. "Awesome! Mom, that is so cool—I can really come with you?"

"Uh-huh," Mom said, chuckling softly.

"So there," Sandy said, sticking her tongue out at me. "Now who's jealous?"

I sat there and didn't say anything. I was glad for Sandy. She'd have a ball in D.C., going to science museums, visiting NASA, and jogging past the White House (she's a star on the school track team).

And I could prepare for my ocean research voyage in peace.

I only hoped the diving suit and the zapper would be ready on time—and would perform the way they were supposed to. If not . . . well, I didn't even want to think about that.

The following Tuesday, Bud, Yo and I met at four a.m. at the Shopton Bay Marina, and boarded a small dinghy that took us out into the bay, where the Swift

Enterprises research vessel *Nestor* was waiting.

Bud gripped the seat with both hands as the little dinghy rocked forward and back. He looked terrified.

"What's the matter with you?" Yo asked him. "Haven't you ever been on a boat before?"

Bud's eyes shifted left and right. "Um, not really," he said. "Does a rowboat on the lake count?"

Oh, boy, I thought. *Maybe inviting Bud and Yo along wasn't such a great idea.*

Oh, well. It was too late to turn back now.

The sky was still dark as we climbed aboard the *Nestor*. But in the east, there was a faint hint of purple—the dawn on its way.

"This ship is so *small!*" Yo whispered.

"It's not a cruise ship, Yo," I reminded her. "It's a research vessel. See all the radar dishes?"

"Cruise ships have those too," she said.

"Don't expect cruise ship food, either," I warned her.

"No?"

"No. It's probably more like the school cafeteria."

"Eeeew!"

I shook my head. If Yo was really expecting a cruise, she was going to be bitterly disappointed.

I worried about Bud, too. He was all excited about the research, but he'd never been at sea before. I was afraid he might get seasick.

I myself had been on the *Nestor* once, but not for a sail. As far as I was concerned, this trip was going to be totally awesome.

And the best part was, I didn't even know what our mission was!

Oh, I knew *my* mission—to test my shark zapper and diving suit under real-life, deep-ocean conditions. I'd been making changes to the suit's control panel for the past week—fixing the damage and moving it to the abdominal area for easier access. I'd had to rig it all in a hurry, too. I only hoped I would get a chance to try it out on this trip.

But I had no idea what my dad was up to. He had refused to tell me, saying he couldn't talk about it until we were safely out at sea. He did mention that it was a deep-water mission, though, and that was all I needed to hear.

See, I knew that when my dad said he was going on a deep-ocean voyage, he meant he'd be going down into the abyss with Swift Enterprises' newest submersible, the *Jules Verne-1*. Dad didn't know it yet, and neither did Bud or Yo, but my plan was to go down with him.

I hadn't told him my plans in advance, of course. If I had, he might have said no.

Anyway, now that we were on board the *Nestor*, I was more than curious to know what the actual mission was.

The door to the bridge area above us opened, and out stepped a suntanned, middle-aged man with a trim white beard. He introduced himself as Captain Walters.

"Hi," I said, shaking his hand. "Um, is my dad here yet?"

He looked up at the helipad that sat above and astern of the bridge. "Mr. Swift will be arriving in a few hours," he said. "He said he had to attend an important meeting in New York City."

"Ah," I said.

Totally typical of Dad. He's incredibly hard to keep up with. It would be really great if we could spend the next two days together on the ship, getting in some quality father-son time.

But I doubted it would happen. He'd always be too busy. That was the real reason I'd wanted Yo and Bud along—to keep me company.

"Why don't we get you kids settled in?" the captain said. "Then I'll show you around the ship."

"Uh, don't you have to drive it?" Bud asked.

I nearly cracked up, but I didn't want to embarrass him.

Like I said, he'd never spent much time on the water.

"I do take the helm coming in and out of port," Captain Walters said. "Once we're out on the open ocean, I'll turn it over to one of the mates." He chuckled. "There's a lot more to do on this ship than drive. You'll see. Come on with me."

He led us through a hatch and down a steep set of stairs to the hold. "Here are your beds," he said, showing us a stack of three bunks that would be our home for the next two nights.

"Get yourselves settled in, and I'll be back in five minutes." Pointing down the passageway, he said, "The head's down there, if you need it." The captain walked off quickly, leaving us to ourselves.

"The 'head'?" Yo repeated.

"The bathroom, Yo," I told her.

"Huh. They don't call it that on a cruise ship."

Then she looked over our sleeping arrangements. "I claim the top bunk!" she said, throwing her duffel bag over Bud's head.

It landed right where she wanted it to. *Of course* it did. Yo is an amazing athlete. You know that event in the Olympics, the decathlon, where you compete in ten different sports? She could win that. From softball, to tae kwon do, to the duffel bag throw, she's got it down.

And Bud? Ah . . . no. Not really.

"You want the middle bunk?" I asked him.

"You don't mind?"

"Nah, go ahead—I don't care."

He was silent for a moment. Then, "Hey, Tom?"

"Yeah, Bud?"

"Why do you think they call it the 'head'?"

"I have no idea."

Yo giggled. "Maybe it's because when landlubbers like Bud get seasick, they spend a lot of time with their *heads* in the *toilet*."

"Not funny," Bud said, but it was too late. Yo and I were already laughing our heads off.

37

Captain Walters was as good as his word. Five minutes later, we were getting the grand tour of the *Nestor*. "We'll start off with the galley," he said, leading us down a short flight of stairs.

Bud looked puzzled. "'Galley'?"

"It means the kitchen," I explained.

"I knew that," he said, nodding like he was Mr. Cool. "Yeah. Smells good. What is that, pancakes?"

"That's right," said the captain. "Chowtime's at oh-five-hundred. That's in about . . . ohh . . ." He checked his precision watch. "Fourteen minutes, twenty-five seconds."

Next he led us down another flight of steps to the engine room.

"Whoa!" Bud said, examining the huge rack of hydrogen fuel cells that powered the ship. "What are those?"

Yo was silent, listening to the whir of the turbines.

"That's our power supply," Captain Walters said. "We've got enough power down here to navigate even in major storms."

"We're not expecting any of those, are we?" Yo asked, looking suddenly anxious.

"Uh, no," said the captain. "Not really."

"What do you mean, 'not really'?" Bud asked.

"Well, there is a storm off the coast of Florida, but it's not supposed to get here for about three days. We should be back in port by then, if everything goes as planned."

I have been on enough scientific missions to know that things rarely go totally according to plan. For instance, my dad's arrival was already delayed.

After the engine room, it was back on deck, where we saw the *Nestor*'s crane lifting the *Jules Verne-1*—or the "Swift-mersible," as I call it—onto the mother ship.

"What is *that*?" Yo asked.

"It's the *Jules Verne-1*," I said. "It's been a major project at Swift Enterprises for the past two years. It's supposed to be the first of a series, each one larger and more capable than the previous model. For instance, the prototype, the *Jules Verne-0*, is a one-seater that can dive to fifteen thousand feet. This one can carry a crew of four to a depth of up to twenty thousand feet."

This was going to be *Jules Verne-1*'s first actual dive, but I didn't mention it to Bud or Yo. I figured, why worry them?

What did it matter, anyway? Everything would go just fine. The submersible would work perfectly, just as it was designed to do.

In theory, at least.

Why did those words keep repeating themselves in my brain? And what was that queasy feeling I got whenever they did?

I'm not usually afraid of the unknown. You can't be if you're a scientist. But I couldn't shake the sense that something terrible was about to happen.

Much to our surprise, breakfast was delicious—even Yo said so.

Scully, the ship's cook, told us he used to be the short-order cook at a "greasy spoon" in Rhode Island.

His pancakes were awesome, and we ate more than our fill—especially Yo. The way she can pack in the food is amazing!

Anyway, it was shaping up to be a beautiful day. The sun had risen, and the water was as smooth as glass on Shopton Bay as we cast off.

The bay is pretty huge, and it took nearly an hour to reach the point where the bay's waters gave way to the open ocean. We knew we were there, though, because all of a sudden, the boat started rocking.

At first it was just swells, but they kept getting larger and larger. Then, as we passed the cape at the head of the bay, the wind kicked up something fierce, and the swells became waves—great big ones with deep troughs between them.

The captain—who was at the helm himself, I noticed—had us pointed directly into the chop. The boat rose and fell, rose and fell, rose and fell . . .

And so did all those pancakes we'd eaten.

The three of us were standing at the port rail, staring out at the shifting horizon. A pod of bottlenose dolphins were racing with us, leaping and smiling their amazing smiles as they leaped out of the waves and plunged back in.

It didn't seem to bother them that we were being rocked back and forth like a cradle gone wild.

The first wave of nausea took me by surprise. I had to fight not to lose my pancakes right then and there. It took a couple more big waves before I began to get used to the pitch and roll. After that, I was okay.

I wondered about Bud, though—this being his

first time at sea. But obviously I had nothing to worry about. He was laughing and whooping each time a wave crested the bow of the boat, and every time we slammed down hard.

"HAHAHAHA!!!!" he cackled. "This is better than the best roller coaster! Bring it on, King Neptune! It's me, Ulysses, King of the World! WHOO-HOO!"

Wow. Who would have thought it? Bud had the cast-iron stomach of a born sailor.

"*Auugggbhh . . .*"

Bud and I both turned to look at Yo. She looked distinctly green.

"Why . . . did I eat those . . . pancakes . . . *aauugbhh . . .*"

Bud and I turned away as the inevitable happened. When Yo had finished losing her pancakes, we helped her down the stairs and up into her bunk. "Cruise ships never rock like this," she said. "I think this boat is gonna sink. . . . Aughh . . ."

That was all Bud had to hear. After he had been made fun of all morning because he was a "landlubber," it turned out *Yo* was the one who couldn't handle it when the going got tough!

It was a rare moment, and Bud wasn't going to let it go without some serious payback. "I wonder what time

42

lunch is served," he started. "Hmmm . . . let's see. . . . Here's the menu. . . . We've got soft-boiled eggs . . . creamed spinach . . . ooo, and sushi! Mmmm . . ."

"Aughhh! Cut it out, you beast!" Yo begged.

I have to admit, I couldn't resist making a few comments myself. I mean, Yo had been bragging about her experiences at sea ever since that afternoon in the ice cream parlor. Besides, we knew she would get back at us sooner or later. She always seemed to get the last word in somehow.

Lunch was served at noon, but none of us wanted to eat. I wasn't totally immune to the boat's rocking and swaying, even if I didn't show it as much as Yo. As for Bud, he showed no signs of slowing down, but I noticed he didn't go to the galley either.

The waves just kept coming. At about three in the afternoon, Captain Walters came below to check up on us. "Everybody okay down here?" he asked.

"I'm dying . . . ," Yo moaned. From the way she looked, it wasn't that hard to believe.

"Gee, I'm sorry," the captain said. "You boys okay?"

"We're fine," Bud said, smiling broadly and saluting. "Just perfect. Great day for sailing."

"I should have warned you about the swells."

43

"Swells?" Yo repeated. "Swells? This is like a hurricane or something!"

The captain smiled and shook his head. "It's just the effect of that storm down south that I told you about. It's a big one, and it's picking up speed, so the wind and waves are reaching all the way up here. But don't worry—it's still plenty far away. If it ever catches up with us—*then* you'll see some waves."

"Could . . . could that really happen?" Yo asked, in a pleading voice.

He looked at Yo and rubbed his chin. "It's weather, so you never can tell." He shrugged. "Sorry about that. I'd offer you a pill for seasickness, but it wouldn't do any good. You have to take it beforehand."

"*Now* you tell me." Yo wiped the cold sweat from her forehead. "Where's that bucket?"

My dad arrived by helicopter at four thirty that afternoon. The big black chopper had a hard time landing on the ship's tiny helipad, because it kept heaving up and down with the waves.

Finally, my dad emerged from the chopper's cabin and came down onto the deck to greet all of us.

"Sorry I'm late!" he shouted over the noise of the

44

chopper blades. He turned back and waved to the pilot, who quickly took off again. Within ten seconds, the helicopter had practically disappeared from view.

"Let me take your bags for you, Mr. Swift," the captain said.

"Thanks, Mark. If you wouldn't mind bringing it into the lab and getting everyone together, I'd like to speak with them all about our mission."

"Very good, Mr. Swift."

My dad is a pretty imposing guy. He's big and tall, and stands straight as a rod. If he wore a uniform, believe me, you'd salute.

"Hello, Bud. Yo, good to see you." He gave me a quick squeeze on the shoulder. "Everything going well, son?"

"Oh, yeah."

"Good. Then let's get started."

He led us down into the ship's lab, the largest space on board. The captain hadn't shown it to us on our little tour, and now I could see why the rest of the ship had seemed so quiet—everyone and his brother was crammed in here.

The whole place was bustling with activity. There

were banks of monitors on every wall. Below them sat a huge set of servers.

In the middle of the room were several computers on desks arranged in a circle. Sitting at each desk were intense-looking scientists, examining charts, videos, maps, and statistics. They dropped what they were doing as soon as my dad walked in.

"All right, everyone," he said, not wasting a single moment. "Bill, could you lower the lights and start the slide show going?"

The scientist named Bill jumped up and hit the light switch. A screen lowered slowly from the ceiling, lit by the glow of the projector.

My dad plugged his laptop into the system, pushed a few keys, and a map of the North Atlantic Ocean lit up the screen.

"This," my dad said, pointing to a spot off the East Coast of the United States, "is where we are right now. This," he moved his hand to the right about a foot, "is where we are headed. It's called 'the abyssal plain.' On one side of it is the continental shelf— shallow water. On the other side, the mid-ocean ridge begins."

"The 'abyssal plain'?" Bud repeated.

"Yes, Bud," my dad said. "It's over three miles deep. That makes it one of the deepest parts of the North Atlantic—except for the Puerto Rican trench, of course, which is a mile deeper."

"Hey! Viva Puerto Rico!" Yo said, perking up a little.

The boat was still pitching and yawing, but by this point she had nothing left in her stomach to lose.

"Viva!" my dad echoed with a smile. "Anyway, the reason we're headed to the abyssal plain, here"—he pointed to a spot on the map—"past the Turner Seamounts, is that it borders on a major earthquake fracture zone. The seamounts themselves are active volcanoes, erupting frequently."

He gave us all a serious look. "Last month, there was an undersea earthquake in this area measuring six-point-zero on the Richter scale. It wasn't felt on land, but instruments detected it. If my calculations are correct, it may be just the first in a series, as this sector of the mid-ocean ridge is still shifting.

"Worst case scenario is a massive quake, followed by a major tsunami. If that happens, the entire East Coast would be in danger. That's why we're here."

"I don't get it," one of the scientists said. "Even if you're right, what can we do about it?"

My dad smiled and opened one of the dozen or so metal suitcases the helicopter had dropped off with him. It looked exactly like the one I'd brought to the aquarium that night the week before. Inside the case was a spherical object with cables emerging from one side.

It was made of the same material I'd used to make my deep-sea diving suit, except it had a more silvery color. It shimmered in the dim light of the lab.

Titanium-laced—of course! I had to give it up for Dad. As good as my idea was, he had already improved on it.

"This," he told us, "is a seismic sensor, specially designed to resist deep-ocean pressure. We're going to be heading down to the bottom of the abyssal plain in the *Jules Verne-1*. We'll put the submersible through its paces, study the deep-ocean faults to find the best locations, and then lay down a linked network of these sensors. That way, if the worst happens, at least we can get a tsunami warning out to people living along the shoreline."

"Wow!" Bud said in a whisper. "This is way cool. Wait till I write it up in the *Gazette!*"

"I told you you'd get a good story out of this trip," I said. "But remember—the *Jules Verne-1* is still not ready for commercial sale. You can't go into detail about it, or the sensors, or my suit, or my zapper, or any of it."

"Tom," he said, giving me a look. "How many times have we had this conversation?"

He had me there. I'm always telling him to stick to the basics and not to give away any of Swift Enterprises' trade secrets. But he's always been great about it. His stories in the *Gazette* are masterpieces—they tease the reader without giving very much away. I'm telling you—that kid is gonna be a famous author someday.

My dad finished his talk. The scientists broke into working groups to prepare for the launch of the *Jules Verne-1*, which was scheduled for the next morning at eight. By then, the captain explained, the storm was supposed to head northeast and break apart, leaving calmer seas that would be perfect for diving.

At six, they called us for dinner. Bud and I went

down to the galley, but Yo was still too sick. She lay in the bottom bunk—*my* bunk—unable even to climb up to her own.

"This one's closer to the bathroom," she said as she closed her eyes.

"It's the head, Yo," Bud corrected her.

"Not funny, Bud," she said, groaning one more time.

He laughed. "Come on, Tom," he said, clapping me on the shoulder, "let's go get us some chow."

4

Dangers of the Deep

It's hard to eat your dinner when it keeps sliding all over the table and your hand keeps missing your mouth with the fork. With the ship pitching and yawing like crazy, it was even harder to keep the food down once we ate it—at least, for me.

Bud seemed to have no problem. He even asked for seconds.

"Hey, Tom," he said after we were done eating and had packed a doggie bag for Yo, even though we knew she'd probably never touch it, "let's go out on deck and check out the stars."

"Are you crazy?" I asked. "You're liable to get tossed overboard. Remember, you're not used to walking around on a heaving ship."

"I could get used to it real quick," he said.

I could tell he was serious. Bud was falling in love with the ocean. I wondered how much he'd still love it if that storm ever got really close to us.

I went out on deck with him—just long enough to get a fantastic glimpse of the Milky Way. Out at sea, you can really see it clearly—a cloud of stars spilling across the top of the sky. Most other places there's too much light for you to make it out.

After about thirty seconds out on the heaving deck, I felt myself getting queasy again. The sky seemed to be rocking back and forth, even though I knew it was *us* doing the rocking. "I'm going back inside," I said. "You're on your own, dude."

"That's cool. See you downstairs."

"Below," I corrected him. "At sea we say 'below.'"

"Oh, do we? Since when did you join the Navy?"

He had me there. I laughed and went back inside.

I could see I didn't have to worry about Bud out on deck alone with the boat rocking like a toy in a bathtub. He was having the time of his life.

I passed through the hatch and walked down the passageway toward the lab, where I knew I'd find my dad. Sure enough, he was seated in front of the bank of computers, working out calculations with two other people—a woman and a man, both wearing Swift Enterprises shirts.

"Dad?" I said as I poked my head in the doorway. "Can I talk to you for a minute?"

"Tom! Come in," he said. "Do you know Bruce and Holly? They're going to be coming with me on the dive tomorrow."

"Uh, that's what I wanted to talk with you about, Dad."

"Oh?" He seemed surprised. "Well, then?"

"Um, it's kind of . . . private," I said, embarrassed.

"I see."

"That's fine, Mr. Swift," said Holly. "Come on, Bruce, how about that cup of coffee?"

They left the lab, headed for the galley.

I was grateful to Holly for her sensitivity. This was my best chance, and I needed to have Dad to myself.

"What's up, son?" He swiveled around in his chair and looked up at me, curious.

"About the dive tomorrow," I began. "I'd . . . well, I'd like to come with you."

"Oh, now, I don't—"

"Wait, let me tell you why!" I said, and proceeded to tell him all about my diving suit and my Swift Kick Shark Zapper, and how important it was for me to take this opportunity to test them out.

My dad listened patiently, nodding slowly. "I see," he said. "Well, Tom, it sounds like you've done a lot of good work, developing the suit and zapper to where you've gotten them."

"Thanks!" I said happily. Praise from my dad isn't always easy to come by.

"And I see what a great opportunity this must be in your eyes," he went on. "But I'm afraid it's out of the question this time."

"What? But—"

"I'm sorry, son, but this mission is urgent. Tens of thousands of lives could be lost if we don't deploy this warning system in time."

"But there are only three of you going down in the *Verne-1*! It seats four! Why couldn't I go down with you and try out the suit and zapper while you deploy the seismic sensors?"

"Because the sensors will take up all the unused space," he said. "There are twelve of them, remember?"

He was right. I'd forgotten about the devices

they'd be carrying along with them. Each one wasn't very big, but twelve of them together would take up as much room as a human being, if not more.

There would be no room for me on board—no chance for me to try out my latest inventions.

I was totally crushed.

"This trip won't be a waste of time for you, Tom," my dad said, reading my thoughts. "You'll be able to help in the control room. You'll be part of our vital lifeline."

"But Dad! Couldn't I go instead of—"

"Instead of Bruce or Holly? I'm afraid not, son. Bruce is a seismic geologist, and Holly's a deep-ocean expert. I'll need both of them with me down there."

"But—"

"No buts," he said firmly. "You know, when I first planned this dive, I did think about taking you with me. But then I decided against it—not because of Bruce or Holly, either. There was . . . there was another reason."

"Huh? What reason?"

"It's too dangerous," he said. "*Jules Verne-1* is a brand new ship, and we're exploring an active seismic zone. There are boiling vents down there, underwater volcanoes—not to mention the fact that a major earthquake could happen at any time."

"Dad . . . are you sure it's okay for *you* to go down?"

"I'm sure it's worth the risk," he said. "Now go get some rest. We've all got a big day ahead of us tomorrow."

I reached down and hugged him. "Good night, Dad."

He patted me on the back. "Don't worry, son. Everything will be fine."

I went back down the passageway to our sleeping quarters, hoping my dad knew what he was doing.

But somewhere deep inside, it just didn't feel right. I was getting that queasy feeling again, and it wasn't just the waves.

I knew as well as he did that in our business, nine times out of ten, things didn't go right the first time. And with this kind of dive, there was zero margin for error.

Yo was lying awake in the middle bunk, groaning softly. I felt sorry for her, and a little guilty, too, for asking her to come along. But honestly—if I'd known she'd get this sick, I never would have brought her.

Bud came up behind me. Obviously, he'd been out on deck the whole time I was with my dad. "You should see the stars," he told Yo as he climbed up onto the top bunk—the one that was supposed to be hers.

"I'm already seeing them, with my eyes closed," she said.

"You want some food?" Bud asked. "We brought you—"

"No thanks!" Yo said quickly. "Let's . . . let's talk about something else."

It was dark in the hold. The only lights were along the floor, where tiny bulbs lit up the passageway using hardly any of the ship's precious energy supply.

I lay down in my bunk, totally frustrated.

"So what time are you going down in the submersible?" Bud asked me.

"I'm . . . not going."

"What?" Yo sat up, forgetting for the moment how sick she felt. "How come?"

"No room in the submersible. My dad wants me to help out in the control room."

"Man," Bud said. "What a letdown."

"It's okay," I said. "The control room's an important

job. There'll be other chances to test out the suit and the zapper."

"What about *us*?" Yo asked. "Can we at least watch you in the control room?"

"I think there's plenty of seating in there," I said.

"Cool," she said. "And no more waves tomorrow, right?"

"That's what the captain said," I replied.

"Thank goodness!" She lay back down and closed her eyes again.

Bud leaned over the edge of his bunk, so that his head was only a foot or so from Yo's. "You know," he said, "I was reading up on this part of the ocean before we left. And it said that in choppy weather, gigantic eels sometimes rise to the surface and slither onto ships to eat people."

"Quit it!" Yo said, sitting up in a hurry. "They do not. You're just making that up, fool."

"That's what the book said," Bud insisted, rolling back up and into his bunk.

"What book?" Yo demanded.

"The book of . . . slithery sea creatures!"

As he said it, Bud dangled something down onto

Yo's face. It took me a second to figure out that it was just a belt.

Yo screamed, and batted it away. "AAAHHH!! Get it away from me!"

Then she realized Bud was just messing around. She reached up, hoisting herself high enough to punch him in the arm.

"OW!" he said, laughing. "What? What'd I do?"

"Cut that out!" Yo yelled, totally forgetting she was seasick.

"Hey, both of you," I said. "Calm down, okay? We can't afford to be goofing around on this trip."

I was thinking of my dad and what he'd said at the end of our conversation. I wasn't much in the mood for fun.

We settled back into our bunks. The waves seemed to be calming down now. The gentle rocking motion was enough to make me sleepy, but not enough to trouble my stomach any more.

"What do you think they'll find down there?" Bud wondered. "Are there any fish that far down?"

"Oh, man," I said. "There are some really weird monsters down there. You ever hear of the *Alvin*?

That submersible from Woods Hole Institution that got written up in *National Geographic* years ago? Well, when the *Alvin* went down to eleven thousand feet, they found all kinds of weird stuff—huge tube worms, giant sea stars—"

"What, is everything giant down there?" Yo asked.

"Not everything," I said. "But I left out the biggest thing of all—the giant sea squid."

"There are giant squids down there?" Bud asked. "I thought those were just a myth."

"They used to think so," I said. "Up till a year ago all they'd seen were pieces that washed up on beaches or got hauled up in fishermen's nets. Then this team of researchers came out with a video, proving giant squids are real."

"How big are they?" Yo asked.

"Even bigger than whale sharks?" Bud asked. Of course, he *would* know what the biggest animal on Earth is.

"Even bigger. More than fifty feet long, with twenty-foot tentacles! They may get even bigger—they've only captured one specimen on videotape so far."

"Really?"

There was a funny, wavering tone in Bud's voice. At first I didn't recognize it, but it sounded a little like—fear!

Yo sensed it right away. "*Now* who's scared?"

I couldn't see well enough in the dark to be sure, but I could have sworn she was smiling—for the first time since we'd set sail.

"I'm not scared," Bud said. "They don't . . . attack ships, do they?"

"Mmmm . . . possibly," I said. "They've found whales with gigantic sucker marks. If our ship looked enough like a whale—"

"It might, to a giant squid," Yo pointed out.

Bud was silent.

"Bud, you okay, dude?" I asked.

"Uh-h-h-huh."

"Oh, *he's* not scared," Yo mocked. "Whassa-madda, did the sea monster eat you all up?"

"I'm *not* scared," Bud muttered.

Yo and I had a good laugh. I was glad she was over her seasickness.

The ship's rocking was gentler now. Pretty soon it got really quiet down in the dark hold. We were all exhausted. Trying to keep your balance—and your lunch—on a boat that's being tossed around in high seas, takes a lot of energy.

Pretty soon I heard Yo snoring softly. Then Bud chimed in too. He . . . well, he sounded a lot like a raging hippo, to tell you the truth.

I lay awake in my bunk for a long time, thinking. In the morning my dad would be going down to the bottom of the sea, on a mission so dangerous he refused to let me come along.

I couldn't stop worrying about him. If something bad happened down there, what would I do—what *could* I do—to save him?

Aw, cut it out, I told myself. Nothing bad is going to happen. Of course it won't. Dad will be just fine.

The *Jules Verne-1* was a precision-built machine, after all. It would do exactly what it was supposed to do.

I was *sure* of it.

But if I was so sure, then why couldn't I fall asleep?

5

The Big Dive

Finally, I did drift off to sleep—only to dream I was being strangled by a horrendously ugly giant squid!

Or was it my *dad* who was being strangled?

No, it was me. . . . The squid had me in its clutches, and it was shaking me. . . .

"Tom, wake up."

My dad's voice.

I sat up so fast, I nearly hit my head on the bunk above me. The giant squid vanished, and there was my dad, standing by the side of the bunk.

"Is it time?" I asked him, rubbing the sleep from my eyes.

"Almost. Go ahead and get washed up, and I'll see you on deck." He turned to go.

"Dad?"

"Yes, son?"

I hesitated. I wanted to tell him not to go ahead with the dive, but I couldn't figure out a good reason—other than my bad feelings and my nightmare. "Um . . . how's the weather?" I finally asked.

He gave me a thumbs-up. "Perfect. See you in ten minutes?"

I nodded, and he hurried off. I reached for my bag and pulled out a fresh shirt.

"Tom? Aren't you forgetting something?"

I looked down at the shelf next to my bed. My wristwatch, which I'd put there before I'd gone to sleep, was talking to me.

"Hello, Q.U.I.P.," I said.

Q.U.I.P. stands for Quantum Utilizing Interactive Processor. In plain English, it's a computerized artificial intelligence—and it lives inside my watch.

I can use Q.U.I.P. to interface with any of the servers at Swift Enterprises, as well as supercomputers at U.S. government research labs and other agencies. He's kind of like a PDA with an IQ of two thousand—*and* a sense of humor.

I call him my "back-up brain," but Q.U.I.P. likes to refer to himself as "the *real* brains of the outfit."

Oh, yes—he speaks. *A lot.* He's got a hundred different voices too. I designed him that way—to pick up on my mood and adjust to it. He really keeps me entertained, I'll tell you.

"What's going on?" Bud murmured, yawning.

"They're going to launch the submersible," I said, strapping on my wristwatch.

"Wha? The sun's not even up yet."

"I guess they're in a hurry. They must want to launch the *Verne-1* while the sea is calm."

"Wait, I'm coming with you."

Bud clambered down out of his bunk—stepping right on Yo's hand.

"*Yeeeoooww!!*" She shrieked, sat up, and smacked Bud on the arm. "That hurt!"

"So did that!" he said, rubbing the sore spot. "What'd you hit me for?"

"I didn't know it was you—I was asleep!" Yo shook

her hand back and forth. "What'd you step on my hand for?"

"It was an accident," Bud said. "I didn't know it was there."

"You ought to look before you go stepping on things," she said.

"Boy, you sure are grouchy in the morning," Bud said.

"It's not morning," she said. "It's pitch-black outside. Look through the porthole."

"Would you two guys cut it out?" I said. "We've got to get moving if we're going to see the launch."

Before you knew it, we were all rushing to make it out on deck in time. No one wanted to miss this moment. The entire crew was out on deck, along with the dozen or so research scientists.

We watched as one of the crewmen maneuvered the *Nestor's* crane into position, then lowered the winch. Another member of the crew attached the hook to the top of the *Verne-1*.

My dad turned to the captain and shook hands. "Well, this is it, Mark," he said.

"Good luck, Mr. Swift," the captain said.

"Thanks. We'll be counting on everyone up here, so good luck to all of us."

Then Dad spotted me. "Tom, you'll be working with Dr. Fletcher in the control room, monitoring our fuel and oxygen levels, and keeping track of our location as we place the seismic sensors along the sea floor."

"Right," I said. I knew the Swift-designed control systems pretty well—operating them wouldn't be difficult.

"See you soon," he said, giving me a quick, tight hug. Then he turned, waved to the crew, and joined his two assistants as they climbed into the submersible.

Captain Walters tightened and sealed the hatch, gave the *Verne-1* an affectionate pat of the hand, and signaled the winch operator.

The bright yellow submersible rose into the air. Then the crane swung around, bringing the *Jules Verne-1* over open water.

The winch was lowered once again. The little yellow sub hit the water with a small splash. The hook was removed, and the crane swung back out of the way.

With a whir and a whine, the *Verne-1* powered up its hydrogen fuel cell array. My dad's face appeared in the porthole. I waved as it sank beneath the surface.

"All right, everyone," the captain said. "All hands to their designated positions. Let's get to work."

I headed for the control room, with Bud and Yo right behind me. Dr. Fletcher, a heavy woman with short gray hair and thick glasses, was there when we arrived.

I knew her from Swift Enterprises—she's been one of Dad's main research assistants ever since I can remember. She found Bud and Yo a comfortable place to sit in an out-of-the-way corner. Then she gave me a nudge. "Come with me, Tom."

I followed her to the far end of the room, where we sat next to each other in front of the bank of readouts.

"There's the submersible," she said, pointing to a sonar blip on a field of green, sinking past depth readouts: one hundred feet, two hundred, three hundred . . .

The *Verne-1* was sinking slowly, carefully—at three miles per hour. At this rate, it would take about an hour for it to reach the bottom.

"Can they hear us?" I asked.

Dr. Fletcher flipped a switch on the control console. "Now they can."

"Dad? Do you read me?" I said.

There was a crackling sound. "Tom? Yes, I read you."

"How's it looking down there?"

"A-okay. Dr. Fletcher with you?"

"I'm here," she said.

"Excellent. All the readouts looking okay?"

"Sure are."

"Well, you're really missing something, Tom," my dad said. "We'll have to get you aboard next time, so you can try out that deep-water suit of yours."

"Yeah," I said. "Sure thing."

Why did he have to go and remind me? Now I was all bummed out again. My dad goes off on a great adventure, while I'm stuck here, staring at a screen.

A half hour later, with everything humming along, I wandered over to Bud and Yo. "Having fun?" I asked them.

"Man, this is *boring*," Bud said. "There's no live camera to look at the fish, or anything."

"Actually, there is," I told him. "But they won't be using it until they're down at the bottom—this isn't a mission to study mid-depth sea life, after all."

"So, what's there to see down at the bottom?" Yo asked. "Giant sea squids?"

"Maybe," I said. "But it's really dark down there. All the camera can show is whatever swims into its searchlight."

"Well, how long will it be till they turn on the camera?"

"Another half hour or so," I said.

"Aw, man! What are we gonna do till then?" she complained.

"Hey, Yo," Bud said, "I'm about ready for breakfast. You?"

Yo's eyes lit up. "Yes! I'm so hungry I could eat a sea monster!"

And why not? She hadn't been able to get any food down since we'd set sail yesterday morning.

"How 'bout you, Tom—you hungry?" Bud asked.

"Bring me a muffin when you come back," I said. "I don't want to leave my post."

I returned to my seat, and checked all the readouts. The submersible was down to ten thousand feet—almost two miles deep. The gauge measuring external water pressure was well into the "danger" zone. Of course, the *Verne-1*'s titanium hull had been built to withstand even greater pressures. It would hold up. I was sure of it.

Twenty-five minutes later, Bud and Yo returned, bearing a blueberry muffin and coffee for me. "Thanks," I told them. "Put it down over there—far away from the electronics."

Just then Dad's voice came over the speaker system. "We have the bottom in view," he said. "Easing submersion rate to five feet per second . . . four . . . three . . . two . . . one . . . and . . ."

There was a thudding sound on the speaker. "We have contact with the bottom, a soft landing at 6:24 a.m. Confirmation?"

"Confirmed," Dr. Fletcher said, reading the monitors intently. "All systems intact."

"That's great," my dad's voice boomed out.

"Hey, Mr. Swift," Bud said, "what's it like down there?"

"Hello, Bud. Well, what we can see from here—which isn't very much—is a sort of cliff made of extruded volcanic matter. It's about a hundred feet high, and doesn't look too stable either."

"Shouldn't you move to safer ground?" Yo asked.

"No, we're in the perfect place to deploy one of the seismic sensors. We're going to do that right now, in fact. Signing off for a minute."

"Hey," Yo asked, turning to me. "How can they do that? Doesn't the sub have to open its door to deploy something? And how can it do that without the water rushing in?"

"All subs have a double hatch," I explained. "It functions as an air lock, and it's pressurized. They enter through the inner hatch, set the seismic monitor on the robot arm, and go back inside. Then the outer door opens, and the arm extends and deploys the device. It's simple, really."

"Ha," Yo said. "If it was really that simple, anybody could do it."

About fifteen minutes later, my dad's voice came on again. "First device deployed," he said. "We are now going to skirt the sea bottom for about five miles to the northwest before deploying the second device. We'll be skirting the edge of that ridge I was telling you about."

"The camera!" Yo reminded me.

"Right. Dad, can you switch on the camera so we can see what you're seeing?" I asked him.

"Sure thing, son."

Dr. Fletcher turned on the big monitor, and

moments later we were staring at the volcanic rock wall my dad had been telling us about. The *Verne-1* appeared to be moving along the wall.

In the glow of the submersible's lights, we could see huge blue tubes with tentacles sticking out of the cliffside, waving in the current. "Tube worms," I said. "They feed off the sulfuric acid that leaks from active deep-sea vents."

"Awesome!" Bud whispered, staring at them in fascination.

Suddenly the entire scene on the monitor exploded in a cloud of what seemed like dust— except it couldn't be dust, because it was at the bottom of the ocean.

"What the—?" I heard my dad's voice come over the system. I heard screams from his crewmates. Then—

"Earthquake!!" my dad yelled.

At that very instant, sirens started blaring all over the control room, as all the readouts went haywire at once. Dr. Fletcher stared at the monitor. "Oh, my," she said. "It's massive . . . massive!"

She leaned over and pressed a button activating the ship's loudspeaker system. "Secure the ship! Code red! We have an under-sea quake in progress! Batten down all hatches!"

"Wait!" I yelled. "What about the submersible? What about my dad?"

She looked at me with panic in her eyes. I could see that she had no idea what to do—so I took matters into my own hands.

"Dad! Dad! Do you read me?"

There was the crackling of static. "Tom . . . can't . . . maneuver . . . avalan—"

The transmission cut off abruptly.

"Tom—the sub's camera!" Bud said, putting a hand on my shoulder.

He was right. While I'd been occupied, there might have been video capture of what had happened to the submersible. "Dr. Fletcher!" I said, shaking her out of her stunned condition. "Can you run back the video capture?"

She nodded blankly, leaned over and pressed some buttons, then pointed at the big monitor. We saw the black cloud erupt from the volcanic wall, just as we had seen it live . . . then nothing for several seconds.

Finally the murk began to clear . . .

. . . and the cliff was *gone*!

In its place was a slope of shattered rubble, reaching nearly as high as the camera itself.

I knew the camera was mounted atop the *Jules Verne-1*, and I also had a pretty good idea of what my dad had been trying to say. The sub had been caught in an underwater avalanche, and he was trying to maneuver it away from danger!

"Dad! Dad, do you read me!" I tried once more.

This time only static answered me.

"Any live video coming through?" I asked.

"Nothing," Bud said.

"Do we have a location for the sub, Dr. Fletcher?"

She started checking her readouts. "Yes, here we are," she said.

"What if they're trapped down there? What are we going to do?"

I could hear the panic in my own voice. I knew I had to calm down—and fast—if I wanted to help save my father.

Dr. Fletcher looked at me and shook her head. "It was a six-point-five on the Richter scale, Tom. This was the quake your father was trying to warn people about. It could spawn tsunamis all along the East Coast!"

Dr. Fletcher bent over her shortwave radio. "Coast Guard, this is research ship *Nestor*, off the Turner Seamounts. Come in, please!"

"Coast Guard monitor zero-one-five-four-nine, go ahead, *Nestor*."

"Reporting an undersea quake, magnitude six-point-five. Tsunamis possible. Please alert all appropriate authorities to spread the alarm!"

"Are you sure, *Nestor*?"

"Affirmative!"

"All right, we'll get right on it. Can you give us your exact position, please?"

I couldn't breathe. I felt as if the weight of fifteen thousand feet of ocean water was pressing down on my chest. I needed to get up on deck . . . needed some fresh air . . .

"Hey," Bud stopped me at the door. "If it was such a big earthquake, how come we didn't feel anything?"

He was right. The boat hadn't even rocked.

Suddenly—but right on cue—we were all knocked to the floor as a violent wave hit the *Nestor* head-on!

The lights blacked out, along with every monitor in the control room. Luckily, the emergency lights kicked in immediately, allowing us to find our way out of the control room and up the stairs.

"Wait here until I make sure it's safe," I told Bud and Yo as we reached the open hatch. I stepped through it and inched my way carefully out onto the deck, making sure I had a firm handhold at all times.

It was a gorgeous, sunny day, but the ocean, which had been so calm just an hour ago, was churning madly. It looked like a washing machine in the spin cycle. The *Nestor* was being tossed around in circles, first this way, then that.

Yo, Bud, and I grabbed onto anything sturdy we could find. This was not the usual pitch and roll—the kind we'd had yesterday, the kind that had made Yo so seasick. This was something entirely different, and totally weird.

And next something even weirder happened. The *Nestor* suddenly rose up, riding on the crest of a huge wall of water.

She paused at the height of the wave, suspended for an instant, then sank back down so quickly that for a moment, we were all completely weightless.

I lost hold of whatever I was grabbing onto, and

went spinning across the deck. As I neared the railing, a huge wave crested over the side of the ship.

It swept me up, over the railing. I plunged into the open sea!

6

Castaway

I was underwater. I'd swallowed a ton of seawater.
Panic took over and I thought, *I'm definitely going
to die.*

Then, my survival instinct took over. I flailed my
arms until I broke the surface. I sucked in as much air
as I could, kicking like crazy. I coughed up seawater,
gasped for more air, coughed some more, and so
on—until finally, I just had to float on my back for a
minute or two, until my breathing could return to
normal, and my heart could calm way down.

When my panic started to ease, I let myself go
upright again. Treading water, I looked around for
the *Nestor.*

She was quickly fading into the distance! My heart sank.

Didn't they know I'd been washed overboard?

My panic returned in an instant, my chest pounding so hard I thought it would burst. I went back to floating on my back, my arms and legs all spread out to help me stay bouyant.

Thankfully, the sea was pretty calm again. Pretty amazing, considering we'd just had a major earthquake and possibly the beginning of a huge tsunami. But that's how it is with seismic waves—once the source stops shaking, the waves quickly quiet down.

I wondered how long it would take before someone aboard the *Nestor* realized they'd left me behind. Come to think of it, was the *Nestor* still in one piece, or had she been damaged by the same humongous wave that had thrown me overboard?

Fortunately, I knew that there was a homing beacon in my life vest—complete with high-intensity light, so that I could be easily located, even in the dark, and could stay comfortably afloat until then.

Unfortunately, my life vest was still back on board the *Nestor*! I hadn't worn it since the previous night, when I was out under the stars with Bud, trying to stay vertical on the *Nestor*'s heaving deck.

What I wouldn't have given now to be back there, with my feet firmly planted on something—*anything*!

Anything would be better than floating alone in the middle of the ocean, with nothing on the horizon in any direction.

Now, I'm a fairly good swimmer. On the school team at Shopton High, I do the four-by-one-hundred-meter medley and the four-hundred-meter freestyle. So if I'd seen the *Nestor* out there, I could have gotten to her. But she was no longer on the horizon.

Still, I knew she couldn't be too far away. The captain would try to keep the *Nestor* near the dive site, so they would have a chance to save my dad and the submersible's crew. Once they realized I was gone, they'd deploy a motorized dinghy, one of the two strapped to the *Nestor*'s sides, to find me. I just had to stay afloat long enough to get saved.

I looked around, and to my great relief, saw that there were several pieces of debris floating not too far from me. I swam for them and grabbed hold of the biggest piece I could reach. It was about six feet square and seemed to have once been part of the wooden hull of a boat. By the looks of it, and the other pieces floating nearby, it couldn't have been a very large one—not even close to the size of the *Nestor*. The giant wave must have totally destroyed it.

I wondered who had been aboard and what had happened to them. Had they all been wearing their life vests? I sure hoped so.

I hauled myself up out of the water and onto the piece of wreckage. With my full weight on it, it floated only about two inches above the water.

Well, I had saved myself, at least for the moment. That certainly was worth celebrating. Now, how was I going to get myself *rescued*?

I could not afford to die like this. I had not forgotten that my dad was in danger. The *Jules Verne-1* was sitting there at the bottom of the sea, probably crippled, with a fairly limited air supply.

My dad had mentioned an avalanche—at least, that's what I thought he'd said. Was the submersible buried under a thousand tons of lava rock?

I knew my dad had left me on board the *Nestor* so that I could take charge in an emergency. He had trusted his life to me. But if I was ever going to save him, I had to save myself first.

"Q.U.I.P., I need you," I said to my wristwatch. My *waterlogged* wristwatch.

Nothing. No response at all.

The watch is *supposed* to be waterproof, but you never know what that really means. Getting it wet while washing your hands is one thing; submerging the watch in salt water is another.

I had to get Q.U.I.P. dried out and running again. Using the little ring of mini-tools I always keep in my pants pocket, I took off the back of the watch. I laid both pieces out on the raft, making sure they were secure and didn't slide into the ocean or get blown away by the breeze.

The day was already a hot one. The water was calm, and there wasn't much wind at all. The watch parts dried out pretty quickly in the late morning sun.

Exhausted, I rested for a while to regain what was left of my strength. I lay there on my little raft with my arms outstretched like a dead body, staring out at the ocean . . .

Speaking of dead bodies . . . was I seeing things? Or was that actually a dead body floating toward me?

It was a body, all right—wearing a diving suit and mask, complete with an air tank on its back!

I got a sudden, sick feeling in my stomach. Death is a shocking thing when you stare right at it. And I also knew that, if I didn't find *Nestor* soon, I'd be just as dead.

I paddled my raft closer, then dove into the water and swam a few strokes until I could get hold of the body and bring it back to my raft. I hauled myself up out of the water, then dragged the corpse on board.

"Ooooohhhhh . . ."

I almost fell off the raft. The body was alive!

I took off the diving mask, and saw that it was an older man, about my dad's age. He had a huge, purple bump on his forehead.

"Where . . . am I?"

"You're in the middle of the ocean," I told him. "You got hit by a giant wave. Are you all right?"

"Wave? Where's my boat?"

"You're lying on what's left of it," I said. "But don't worry. I'm going to get us back to my ship."

He groaned and closed his eyes. That bump on his head must have really hurt.

I made sure he didn't have any other injuries that needed attention. Apart from some cuts and bruises he seemed like he'd be okay—if he didn't have internal bleeding, that is—and if we didn't both float away into oblivion.

Staring at the air tank, I suddenly got an idea. "Does that tank of yours have any air left in it?" I asked my wounded companion.

"Should have about fifteen minutes worth," he said. "Oooohhh . . ."

"You just rest," I said. "I'm going to get us out of this mess."

"How?"

"I'm going to use the pressure in your air tank to propel us back to my ship."

If it wasn't already too far away, that is.

First things first, though. I put my watch back together, and held up its solar recharging panel to catch the sun's energy.

Nothing happened, but I kept trying. I knew it would take awhile for enough energy to be converted by the solar panel. Sure enough, five minutes or so later, the watch's digital readout sprang to life.

"URHGNGN . . ." The voice of Q.U.I.P., garbled by salt crystals, emanated from the watch.

"Hello, Q.U.I.P.," I said. "What is your condition?"

"Gzz . . . What happened to me? Everything tastes salty."

I heaved a sigh of relief. If Q.U.I.P. still had his sense of humor, he must be okay. And with his help, I knew we'd come out all right somehow.

"You were submerged in salt water. Q.U.I.P., I need to locate *Nestor*."

"Deploying GPS," it said.

My watch face opened, making a buzzing sound. A tiny titanium radar dish rose from the watch's open face and deployed itself, turning this way and that to locate the nearest GPS satellite. "*Nestor* located."

"Distance?"

"2.3654 miles."

Not too far—by my rough calculations, with fifteen minutes worth of compressed air, we would be able to get at least within sight of the *Nestor*.

"Course?"

"Seventy-five degrees south-southeast."

"You'll have to guide me," I said to Q.U.I.P. "I have no instruments."

"Aren't you counting *me* as an instrument?"

I shook my head in admiration. Had I really been

smart enough to design this tiny work of complete genius?

"A little more to the left," said Q.U.I.P., telling me which way to point the air tank before putting it into action. "And . . . now!"

I hit the valve, releasing the pressurized air in the tank. It worked like a charm and propelled us along at a slow but steady clip. All I had to do was make sure I didn't let go of it—and hope that it didn't run out of air before we found the *Nestor*.

After about fifteen minutes I saw her mast appear over the horizon. "There she is!" I yelled.

The noise woke up my wounded passenger. "Huh?" he said groggily.

"We're saved!" I told him. "You're going to be all right!"

"Thank you." He smiled, then closed his eyes again, exhausted but happy.

"Don't bother to thank *me*," I heard Q.U.I.P. say.

Sometimes I think I made him *too* human.

7

Rescue Mission

The tank ran out of air, but now we were well within shouting range of *Nestor*.

"Tom!" I heard Yo screaming, even as I saw her long arms waving at me. Bud was right next to her on the deck, jumping up and down and raising his arms to the sky in triumph.

The *Nestor* looked damaged somehow, though I couldn't figure out in what way. It was only when I was brought on board, hauled up by the strong arms of two crewmen, that I realized what was wrong.

The ship was listing to starboard. Not terribly, but she was definitely not level anymore.

Or maybe it was me. I was more than exhausted—I was practically in shock from being out in the water for three hours. No, it was the ship. . . . It was definitely tilting to the right.

Captain Walters noticed me looking around, confused. "We've got water in two of the ballast compartments," he said. "Should have it pumped out by tonight."

"Any other damage?" I asked.

Before he could answer, Bud and Yo ran up to me. Yo threw her arms around me in a hug.

"You stupid idiot!" she yelled in my ear. "Why didn't you hold on tighter?" she asked, with tears in her eyes.

There was no good answer. I had been holding on tight—but the wave had been so powerful, it didn't matter. I could have been superglued to the wall, and I *still* would have been washed overboard. But I knew Yo would never believe that.

I could see that the *Jules Verne-1* was not sitting on its mountings aboard the *Nestor*. So it was clearly still down at the bottom of the ocean.

I broke free from Yo. "I'm fine," I said. "Really. It's that other guy who's hurt."

"Who is he, anyway?" Bud asked.

"No idea," I said. "Looks like he was out at sea on his boat, doing some diving, when the quake and the wave hit. It trashed his boat. That's what's left of it down there." I pointed over the side at my raft.

"Okay," Bud said, whipping out his note pad. "I want the whole story, from the minute you hit the water. Man, this is gonna make the front page of the *Gazette* for sure!"

"Maybe later, Bud," I said.

"What are you, a machine?" Yo said, grabbing Bud's notebook out of his hand. "Tom's dad is still down there, remember?"

"Sorry, Tom," Bud said, looking down at his feet.

"I'll tell you all about it when we're safely back in port," I said.

Then I turned to the captain. "Any word from the *Verne-1?*"

The captain shook his head sadly. "Nothing since the last transmission you heard. Our monitors detect no movement and no signal."

I stared at him blankly. It took a few seconds for the meaning of his words to fully sink in.

"You mean . . . ?" I said.

Captain Walters swallowed hard. "They . . . may still be alive somehow," he said. "The submersible has enough air for eight and a half more hours—if her hull is still intact."

"Is there any way to haul them back to the surface if the sub's disabled?" Bud asked.

The captain pointed to a spool of strong, thick cable. "We've got fifteen thousand feet of that," he said. "Assuming we can find the sub. But we'd need someone down there to attach the cable. They can't swim out of the submersible to do it—they'd be crushed by the pressure."

"Can I ask a stupid question?" Yo said.

"Fire away."

"How come the cable wasn't attached to the *Verne-1* in the first place?"

"We had twelve seismic monitors to deploy," the captain explained. "And the submersible was scheduled to explore the entire fracture zone of last month's earthquake. It needed more mobility than it would have had while attached to the cable."

Okay. I'd been listening carefully to everything

the captain said. My brain was processing every word, searching for hope, for some way to save my dad and the others.

So, they needed someone to attach the cable. Well, I had my pressure-proof suit aboard, didn't I? Man, it was a lucky thing Dad hadn't said yes when I'd asked to come along in the *Verne-1*!

Now I had at least a fighting chance of saving his life. But how?

Yes, I could attach the cable, but first we'd have to locate the *Verne-1*. Was I just going to go down solo, hanging onto the cable?

That idea posed a big problem. Even loaded down with two air tanks, I'd only be good for three hours underwater. An hour to get down and an hour to get back up—that left only one hour.

No, I'd need more air than that—a lot more. Because the odds were, I wouldn't find the *Jules Verne-1* waiting for me when I got to the bottom.

After all, it could have been anywhere within a two-mile radius. It would probably take a long time before I found it.

There had to be a way . . .

Then it hit me like a sucker punch—the *Jules Verne-0*!

Yes—the prototype that we'd built last year, when we were still working out the final design. The *Verne-0* was still stored in the warehouse at Swift Enterprises.

Assuming it was undamaged I could use the prototype to get to the sea bottom and save Dad!

"I've got to contact my mom!" I told the captain.

"Mrs. Swift is being tracked down right now," he said. "We wanted to let her know you've been rescued."

Of course. They'd called her when I went overboard. "Did you tell her about my dad?" I asked.

The captain cleared his throat. "Not yet. We thought it was still quite possible that the submersible is all right. They may just have lost their signal."

"No!" I said. "If that was all, you'd still be able to track their movements. The *Jules Verne-1* is not moving, Captain."

I took a deep breath. "I need to talk to my mom right away."

"This way, then." The captain led me up to the bridge, where one of the crew was already speaking to my mom on the ship's satellite link. I took the phone from him.

"Mom!"

"Oh, Tommy, you're alive! I'm so relieved. Are you hurt?"

"I'm fine, Mom. I'll tell you all about it later—but right now, we've got another emergency."

"*Another* one? Good gracious, is your father all right?"

"Mom, I need you to contact Smitty at the warehouse. Tell him to get the *Jules Verne-0* ready for deep-sea testing *immediately*. Tell him to load it inside the Swift Sub-Orbiter."

"Yes, Tom, but what—?"

"Then, Mom, I need you to get someone to fly the Sub-Orbiter out here to the *Nestor* to deliver the submersible."

"Yes . . . but it's just a *prototype*, Tom. It was never intended to—you're not thinking of—?"

"Mom, I can't explain now. Just have them fly it out here as soon as possible, okay? There's not a moment to lose—it's a matter of life and death!"

"Life and—I'm on my way," she said, and hung up the phone.

Wait—did she just say she was on her way?

What did that mean? She wasn't planning on . . . or *was* she?

She *was*.

Three hours later—after I'd had a quick bite to eat, an hour of putting final touches on my deep-sea diving suit, and, finally, an hour of exhausted sleep— the sleek, black Swift Sub-Orbiter came over the horizon.

The Sub-Orbiter is an amazing piece of engineering. It's designed to operate both as a helicopter— complete with hovering and vertical landing—and as a high-speed plane that can soar high enough to leave Earth's atmosphere. We're trying to tweak it so that it can take the place of a space shuttle—but that's a few years off yet.

The Sub-Orbiter came to a stop in mid-air over the *Nestor*, firing its jets forward and backward simultaneously to make the craft hover. It was far bigger than the helicopter that had dropped off my dad the day before. The helipad was way too small for it, but somehow, its pilot steered it into perfect landing position. It touched down, and the engines whined to a stop. Out stepped the pilot, followed by my mom—and my little sister!

Oh, no, I thought. *That's all I need.*

Now, instead of getting ready for my rescue dive, I was going to have to deal with *two* people's emotions—starting with my little sister's hysterical panic.

My mom ran straight over to where I was standing with the captain, and hugged me tight. "Oh, Tom!" she said.

"It's okay, Mom," I told her. "It's going to be all right, don't worry."

"Has there been any word from him?" she asked the captain.

He shook his head. "No, but that doesn't mean—"

Sandy cut him off. "You've got to go down there right away and bring them back up!"

"That's exactly what I'm going to do," I said. "Calm down, Sandy."

"You?" my mom gasped. "Oh, no, Tom—let someone else do it."

"He's *my* dad, not theirs," I said, indicating the members of the crew. "Besides, I know how the submersible works—they don't."

My mom looked deep into my eyes. "What if there's another earthquake, or an aftershock?" she asked. "I can't—I *won't* lose my son, too."

Meaning she thought she'd already lost her husband . . . my dad.

"Don't worry, Mom," I said. "I'll be careful. You'll see, everything will be fine."

She just kept looking at me. "Tom—"

"Trust me, Mom. I'll be okay—and so will Dad."

"I'm coming with you!" Sandy said suddenly.

"No, you're not," I said.

"Yes, I am."

"No, you're not."

"Yes!"

"No."

"YES!!"

"Sandy, stop it!" Mom yelled. I'd never heard her shout at Sandy like that.

Neither had Sandy. This was clearly a special occasion, and it was no time for one of Sandy's childish temper tantrums. I mean, okay, she's a mathematical genius, but nobody ever called her mature for her age.

Sandy sniffed back tears. She and Mom both hugged me hard, as if they were afraid they'd never get another chance.

Meanwhile, the *Jules Verne*-0 had been unloaded

from the Sub-Orbiter and prepared for its descent into the deep.

Now it was *my* turn to get ready.

I turned to Bud, who was carrying my diving suit and the helmet with the zapper. "Ready," I said. "Bud fitted me into the suit.

Before Yo fastened on the helmet, she said, "Don't take any stupid chances."

"Don't worry," I said.

But I didn't say I wouldn't.

I climbed aboard the *Jules Verne-0*. It was so cramped inside that I could barely move around. It would have been nice to have company along for the ride—someone who could operate the submersible while I went outside of it in my diving suit—but there was no possible way. Even if there'd been enough oxygen aboard for two, there was no room in here at all.

The captain's face appeared in the doorway. "Uh, Tom," he said, looking very serious. "There's something else you should know."

"Yes?"

"That storm? The one that rocked us around yesterday? It's changed course, and it's coming straight for us . . . closing in fast. It may even hit us while you're down there."

I looked out the porthole of the *Verne-0* at the southern sky. There were dark clouds creeping over the horizon.

"You might want to reconsider, Tom," he said. "I mean, this is a bad storm, and very fast-moving. If it gets bad enough, being attached by cable to the *Verne-0* might prevent us from steering into the waves. In other words, we may have to cut the cable loose to save the *Nestor*."

I took in his words, nodding slowly. If the cable was cut, I could still bring the prototype back up to the surface on its own power. But there would be no chance then for the *Jules Verne-1*.

On the other hand, if we waited for the storm to arrive and then blow over, it might be too late anyway to save my dad and the rest of the submersible's crew.

"I don't have a choice. It's my dad down there," I said.

He stared at me, and then smiled and nodded. "All right, then. Good luck, Tom."

"Thanks." We shook hands, and then he closed the hatch.

Soon I could hear the sound of the winch swinging around. The big hook was attached to the top of my craft, and I was hoisted into the air.

As the *Verne-0* swung free of the *Nestor* and was lowered past the deck, I saw my mom, Sandy, Yo, and Bud all waving to me with worried looks on their faces.

I gave them a thumbs-up, and then, the *Jules Verne-0* hit the water.

"Here we go," I said, with a sinking feeling.

Into the Deep

I had always dreamed of going on a dive in one of the Swift Enterprises submersibles. But I never thought it would be like this.

Somewhere down there was my dad, using up his last hours of oxygen along with the rest of his crew. And here I was, only now breaking the surface in my last-ditch attempt to save them.

On my wrist, inside my watch, was Q.U.I.P.— hopefully, fully recovered from his salt-water bath. Through the *Verne*-0's communications system, I would be in contact with the *Nestor* at all times.

Still, I felt as alone as I'd ever felt in my life.

I tried not to think about my dad. It would be

more than an hour before I made it all the way to the sea bottom. Even when I got there, my craft would be tethered to that steel cable, so its movements would be limited—making it harder to search for the *Jules Verne-1*.

Before it lost contact with the *Nestor*, the *Verne-1* had already placed one of its seismic sensors. It had been on the move, hunting for a spot to place the second one, when the earthquake struck.

The submersible could have traveled far from its original launch spot. How would I find the *Verne-1* if it wasn't in sight when I reached the bottom?

I would have to communicate my intended movements to the crew back on the *Nestor*, so it could maneuver the ship along with me, making sure the cable had enough play and didn't snap. If it did, there'd be no way to tow the *Verne-1* back up to the surface.

I remembered Captain Walters's last words to me: If the storm hit, as predicted, they might not be able to maneuver with me. They might even have to cut the cable. That scenario spelled doom for my dad and his crew.

My dad's last audible word had been "avalanche."

At least it sounded like that. Was the *Jules Verne-1* buried under rock and mud? Was the crew even alive?

I couldn't think about it any longer. I stared out the prototype's porthole at the incredible creatures of the sea, trying to make the time pass more quickly.

A manta ray was the first thing I spotted. I thought about how, with its twin fins breaking the surface, it would look like a pair of sharks, swimming together to someone surfing or swimming. Totally terrifying. But manta rays are pretty gentle creatures, as long as you don't irritate them or step on them.

A school of striped bonito whisked by again and again. I thought it was an endless stream of fish, until I realized they were circling past my porthole over and over again.

They were chased off by a seven-foot-long white-tipped shark. And then about a dozen bluefin tuna cruised past—probably also hunting the bonito. In the sea, as on land, life eats life in order to live.

"Tom? Do you read me?"

It was Bud's voice, emanating from the speaker built into the prototype's control console. Equalizer lights blipped up and down, registering the timbre and pitch of his voice. The system was built to make adjustments to the human voice, to compensate for the distortion of deep-ocean pressure.

"I'm here," I said. "Man, you're missing some show."

"What do you see?" Yo talking now.

Just then, a sperm whale swam slowly by, accompanied by her calf.

"If I told you, you'd just be jealous."

"I already am, dude," Bud said.

"Come on," Yo added. "Share."

"Okay," I said.

And I did. It kept all of our minds off the danger of this mission—but soon, as the prototype sank deeper into the mid-ocean zone, there were fewer and fewer fish to talk about.

It was dark in these depths, except for the ship's searchlight, which played back and forth across a narrow slice of the view. Anything outside its range was blanketed in total blackness.

"I see a—I see a giant squid!" I yelled.

"Wow!"

"Just kidding, Yo. Stay with me though—there's one out there somewhere, I'm sure."

"I just can't believe a word you say, Tom Swift," Yo muttered.

"Quit messing around, huh?" Bud said. "This is serious business."

As if I needed reminding. "Okay, okay."

Just as I said that, the weirdest creature I'd seen yet floated past my porthole. It looked like a red eel, except it had a crown like a rooster and a big, bright red fin across its top. Below, it trailed two long fins—which acted as bait to draw prey closer. And it was bioluminescent.

Chasing the two "bait" fins was a school of see-through fish with glowing skeletons.

"Well?" I heard Yo say.

"Never mind," I said. "You wouldn't believe it if I told you."

Q.U.I.P.'s tiny radar dish rose from the center of my wristwatch and swiveled toward the porthole. "It's a roosterfish," Q.U.I.P. said. "And those are hatchet fish." He uses his radar as his "eyes"—and it serves him pretty well, too.

"Thank you," I said, "Mr. Know-it-all."

"Thank *you*," said Q.U.I.P., missing the humor in my voice.

The cable kept unwinding, lowering me deeper and deeper beneath the surface of the sea. My gauges told me that I was now at four thousand feet.

It was taking *forever* to get to the bottom! At any moment, my dad could be breathing his last! Couldn't they lower me down any faster?

Of course I knew they couldn't—not without risking snapping the cable or damaging the prototype. Still, it was agonizing.

Outside the porthole, there now appeared an even weirder fish. Only two inches long, it looked like a sharp-toothed lizard sitting on a rock, except that the rock was a part of its body. "Okay, Q.U.I.P.," I said. "What is that?"

The tiny radar dish swiveled at the porthole again. Q.U.I.P. beeped softly, computing the data that was coming across its optical sensor. "Chiasmodon niger. It can swallow prey up to twice its size."

I looked again at the "rock" underneath the "lizard." Obviously, it was the fish's stomach.

"Fierce," I said.

"Fierce indeed."

"What?" Yo's voice came over the speaker. "What now?"

"I couldn't even begin to describe it," I said. "But the prototype is capturing digital video the whole time. You can watch it later—when this is all over."

If I ever get back to the surface, I thought.

"How's the weather up there?" I asked.

"Raining," Bud said. "We're starting to rock again."

"You okay, Yo?" I asked.

"Don't talk about it," she said. "Let's stick to the mission, huh?"

Good idea. Only there wasn't much I could do between now and when my ship hit the bottom.

"Why don't we just give it a rest for a while?" I said. "I'm tired of talking."

"Whatever you say," Bud said.

I sat there in silence, watching the watery world go by in my submersible's searchlights. I couldn't stop thinking about my dad. I wished I'd invented a time machine, so I could make this descent go faster!

The minutes ticked by, and the wait was agony. My submersible had passed through the sunlit zone (from 0-660 feet down), the twilight zone (660-3,300 feet), and the dark zone (3,300-13,200 feet). I was now in the deep abyss, and it was as dark as anyplace on Earth—except, of course, for the narrow beam of light created by my ship's searchlights.

Still the *Verne-0* and I sank downward. Now, out the porthole, I could see a steep volcanic cliff. I knew from the charts we'd studied with my dad the night before that it marked the side of a seamount at the edge of the abyssal plain.

The cliff had jagged edges of newly formed lava rock. Everywhere there were ledges of sand and rubble that looked ready to cascade downward at the slightest shake of the Earth's crust.

I could just picture one of them falling onto the *Jules Verne-1*.

No—can't think about that, I told myself.

My console started beeping, and I scanned the monitor. A jagged green line marked the ocean bottom, a blinking, sinking green light was my tiny ship. The two were getting closer . . . closer . . . and . . .

BANG!

My ship hit the bottom with a thud and a shudder. For a second, I was sure that the groaning sound I heard was the *Verne-0*'s titanium shell buckling from the impact.

But no. After a moment all was silent except the

beeping of the monitors, measuring oxygen flow, power usage, and carbon dioxide levels.

I was at the bottom. *Finally!*

I stared out the Swiftglass porthole at the cloud of sand stirred up by my ship's landing. Slowly, it began to clear.

Nothing.

No *Jules Verne-1*. Just flat, empty sea bottom.

Now what was I going to do?

I flicked on the prototype's holographic ground scanner. In seconds, a 3-D image of the sea bottom around me displayed itself.

This was helpful, but only a little. The scanner could only see what I could illuminate by playing the sub's searchlights over the surrounding terrain. The searchlights were adjustable, but they could only take in fifteen degrees at a time—a very narrow slice of pie.

Where the holographic scanner helped was in collecting the slices as I swiveled the lights, and then, using smart technology, assembling them into an entire three-hundred-sixty-degree, 3-D landscape.

The beauty of having this virtual, holographic landscape in front of me was that I could manipulate it, so that I got the view of the sea bottom from above, seeing past obstacles like rocks and ridges.

It was something I could never have done by myself from inside the vehicle—and something I hoped would help me spot the *Jules Verne-1*.

The ocean bottom was rocky—craggy, even—and mostly covered in black, mucky slime. The only natural light came from the bioluminescent creatures that live down here on the abyssal plain, eating whatever bits of food float down from above.

Eyeless shrimp were hovering outside the sub's two portholes, which had been flattened out by the ocean pressure. On the surface, they bulged outward.

The holographic image seemed to show a ridge of rubble rising from the sea bottom at the far end of my horizon. Above it hovered the cliff I'd seen while being lowered down here.

Could that pile of rubble be covering the *Jules Verne-1*? I sure hoped not—but it was definitely worth a look.

My sub-to-surface video monitor blinked on. *Nestor* was remotely opening the link—draining my craft's precious power to check and see if I was all right.

"I'm fine," I said, "but we'd better not waste energy."

I wanted to conserve every drop of power my ship had left, so I could use it to save my dad and the others.

I could see Bud, Yo, and the captain hovering over their monitor. They all wore worried faces.

"You look green," Yo said.

"It's just the light in here—the glow of the monitors."

"Oh. So . . . you're okay?"

"Yeah."

"Any sign of the *Verne-1*?" the captain asked.

"Not just yet—but I do have a reading I want to go check out."

"Fine. We'll play out the rest of the cable for you—we've still got about two hundred feet."

"That ought to be enough," I said. "I can at least get close to the spot."

"Tom," the captain added, "that storm's getting worse, and fast. We don't have much time to get this done."

"I understand," I said. "We'd better shut the link now. I need to conserve power."

"Okay, then," he said. "We'll check back with you in a little while."

I waited for the rest of the cable to play out, then

maneuvered my craft toward the mound of debris in the distance.

My holographic display changed, shifting to reflect my sub's position. The virtual view was better than staring out the porthole into the dim depths, where everything tended to flatten out.

My tiny submersible had been designed to use as little power as possible. Its hydrogen cell was small and lightweight—the only way it would fit on a craft as tiny as the *Verne-o*. And that meant the ship could only travel at five miles an hour—a speed that seemed impossibly slow right now. Especially since I could only spend four hours down here— three hours outside the *Verne-o*, using the air in my tanks, and one hour inside it (not counting going down and coming up)—before the *Verne-o* itself started running out of air, and I had to head back to the surface.

It was a drop-dead timetable—I couldn't stay down here any longer than that, even if my mission wasn't complete.

I floated past translucent, jelly-like creatures; fish that looked prehistoric but had no eyes (who needed them in this totally dark realm?); and pulsating, hairy worm-like things. I wasn't sure if they'd ever been seen by human eyes before.

Too bad the video link was shut down. If it had been switched on, the scientists back on the *Nestor* would have had a good time looking for new deep-sea species. But this was a rescue mission, and every ounce of power had to be conserved.

I passed close to a rock "chimney"—an undersea volcanic vent. It was belching black smoke straight from the earth's core into the murky water. Attached to its sides were tube-like creatures that looked a little bit like sea cucumbers, but I knew that these animals fed off the sulfurous minerals that belched out of these "black smokers."

These creatures lived, it seemed, not on oxygen like most life we know of, but by breathing in sulfur dioxide instead.

The mound of rubble I was looking for now came into clear, well-lit view. I wanted to circle the entire area in the submersible to get the view from the far side of the mound—but I was now at the very end of the cable's reach and could go no farther.

I tried circling the mound in the other direction. If this didn't work, I had no idea what I was going to try next.

I could, I suppose, power the prototype to the northwest—the direction my dad had said they were going next. The *Nestor* would have to steam in the same direction along with me, at the same speed, so as not to snap the cable. It would be a delicate maneuver, to say the least—especially if the storm was churning up big waves.

I saw nothing in or near the mound. No light or movement at all. No signs of life.

If the *Verne-1* was here, it was completely buried and all was lost.

I tried my sonar, playing it off the side of the mound. Nothing.

Then I tried my high-tech sensors, a last resort before I gave up on this spot and moved on. The sensors were made to detect the chemical signature of the artificial alloys Swift Enterprises had used to make the titanium shell of the *Verne-1* harder and more pressure-resistant.

The sensor blipped once, twice, three times—then started going crazy.

Eureka! I'd found the *Jules Verne-1!*

But where *was* it?

Just then, the sea bottom started to shake and rumble. "Dust" flew up from the ocean floor, and part of the debris mound slid downward, tumbling off the edge of a rock ledge I hadn't noticed before and revealing the faint glow of some large, bioluminescent creature.

Wait . . . no . . . that wasn't bioluminescence. It was . . . it was a porthole!

It was the bow of the submersible!

That meant the *Jules Verne-1* still had power left— which was great news, because that also meant its hull hadn't been punctured, and its resistance to the incredible pressure at these depths was still intact.

But that didn't answer the most important question: *Was its crew still alive?*

9

Buried Alive?

I had found the *Verne-1*. Now came the really hard part of my mission—somehow, I had to get it back up to the surface in one piece.

The submersible appeared to be almost totally buried by the rubble from the undersea avalanche. Its rear portion—the twenty or so feet that was invisible to me, buried under the rock and sand—had to be damaged, if not totally crushed. And that included the ship's communications, air lock, and propulsion system.

Titanium is one of the hardest, strongest substances on Earth, and we'd made it even stronger by combining it with those patented alloys, designed especially for undersea pressures, that my special sensors had detected.

But nothing could have held up to the force of that much rock, multiplied by the sheer depth of the ocean down here on the abyssal plain.

Only the front portion of the *Verne-1*, containing its crew quarters, appeared to be intact. I guessed that my dad had ordered the lights turned on, at the risk of using up the ship's remaining power, in the hope that someone would find them before it was too late.

Well, here I was. I'd found them, all right. But I couldn't get close enough to see through their porthole and determine whether they were still alive. For all I knew, their oxygen might have run out already.

No . . . can't think like that, I told myself. *They just have to be alive.*

The *Jules Verne-1* had begun its dive with enough oxygen for twelve hours of undersea exploration. More than nine hours had already passed. That meant I had less than three hours left to save her.

Assuming there were no leaks, I had every reason to think that the *Verne-1*'s crew was still breathing. But I couldn't tell for sure. And even if I succeeded in freeing the *Verne-1* from the rubble, how would I be able to save its crew if the ship's propulsion system was crushed?

I couldn't fit them on board the prototype, that was for sure—there was barely enough room for me and my diving suit.

No, there was no way they could come on board with me, even if I could somehow dock our two craft together and make the connection air tight.

The only way to do it was to transfer the steel cable from the prototype to the *Verne-1*, so it could be hauled up by the *Nestor's* powerful winch. Once that was done, I could return to the surface inside the prototype under my own power.

However, to do that I would first have to free the *Jules Verne-1* from the volcanic boulders that were piled on top of it. Even wearing my diving suit, it would be impossible to accomplish that by hand.

If you asked me up on the surface how I would tackle freeing a submersible from a mountain of rubble, sand, and minivan-size boulders, I would say, "that's easy—you just rig some explosives to a waterproof fuse, set them off, and away you go."

Unfortunately, I hadn't thought to pack any

explosives aboard the prototype. No fuses, either. Stupid of me, and it was too late now to go back up to the surface to get them.

Then it came to me—I had two air tanks. Each was a canister of pressurized oxygen, together with helium and other inert gases to keep the nitrogen level low. In other words, compressed air, high in oxygen content—a perfect explosive.

Ah, but how to set it off?

"Q.U.I.P.," I asked, "is there anything on board that can ignite even in water?"

"You might try the underwater blowtorch attached to the air-lock hatch."

"Of course!" I gasped. The blowtorch had been included in the ship's inventory in case emergency repairs were needed.

"What about a fuse?" I said. "I'll have to fashion one that will burn underwater. Preferably manganese terfidium sulfate. Any of that on board, Q.U.I.P.?"

"You might use some strips from the lining of the serial ballast levelizer. It should be soft enough to fashion into a long, thin string that will stay lit underwater."

The part of my ship he was referring to was critical

to keeping the *Verne*-0 upright underwater. Without it, the prototype might end up upside down or on its side.

But what other choice did I have?

I went to work. First I steered the prototype far enough away from the *Verne*-1 to be out of range of any explosion I set off.

Then I got busy, stripping a long enough piece of the terfidium padding to make a fuse-like strip about six feet long. I hoped it would burn slowly enough to give me time to get out of range before the air tank blew.

Finally, my improvised explosive device was ready for action. It was time to venture out there, into the pitch-blackness of the deep-ocean floor.

One more thing before I left. It was time to make contact with the *Nestor* and let them know what I was up to. I fired up the power to full strength, making real-time communication possible.

"Hello up there!" I said as the monitor blinked to life. "Anybody home?"

The picture was full of static that came and went, but I could still make out Yo and Bud. The captain was no longer with them, and I could barely hear their responses.

"Tom! . . . storm . . . antenna . . . bad waves . . . going on down there?"

From what they were saying, I figured the storm had worsened and was affecting the ship's antennae. They had already been damaged once, by the big wave that had knocked me off the deck.

"I've found the *Verne-1*!" I told them. "She's intact, and they have power, but she's partially buried. I'm going to try and free her."

". . . did you say?" Bud asked. ". . . they alive?"

"I don't know," I said. "I'm going in now for a closer look."

"Play . . . cable?" Yo was saying.

"I'm going to need all the slack you can give me," I told her. "I'm going to remove the cable from the prototype and attach it to the *Verne-1*. Then I'll contact you to haul them up."

". . . about *you*?" Bud asked.

The static was getting worse. I could barely make them out now, let alone understand what they were saying. I also had to wonder if *they* could make out *my* words.

"I'll be fine," I said. "I'll bring the prototype up on its own power."

At least, I *hoped* so.

"Tell Mom and Sandy not to worry," I said.

Of course I knew that was a stupid thing to say, but I wanted them to know I had confidence in our chances—even if I really didn't.

It made no difference what I said, anyway, because there was now so much static on the line that I was sure they couldn't hear a word of it.

I gave up and flicked off the monitor.

I picked up my improvised explosive device. I would be sacrificing one and a half hours worth of my precious air supply by blowing it up. That would leave me with only the one and a half hours in my other tank and whatever was left of the *Verne-0*'s air supply.

The question, though, was not whether I could afford to lose it. The question was, could I afford not to?

"Tom," Q.U.I.P. said, "you'll have to take me apart again, so you can use your watch as the detonator. That, alas, will be a true loss to you, if you should need my advice afterward."

"I can put you back together again," I told him.

"I hope so—for both our sakes."

He was right about that. "Let's do it," I said.

✦ ✦ ✦ ✦

I rigged the oxygen tank to the timer and fastened it to the fuse. At the other end—my end—I attached my wristwatch, stripped of Q.U.I.P's chip, which I left on the control console. Later on, I would try to revive him by connecting him with the prototype's master server.

I had to attach the cable to the top of the ship, then, hopefully, the force of the explosion would clear away the rubble, freeing the trapped back end of the *Jules Verne-1*. Then I would come back to the prototype and contact the Nestor, telling them to haul the *Verne-1* back up to the surface.

All fine, *in theory*, at least.

But I was now about to leave the safety of the prototype and venture out into open water, with no spare tank of air, and with nothing to protect me but my untested diving suit.

I had worked on it and worked on it. Every adjustment I could think of had been made. It was time to try it out under real-world conditions.

It should work like a charm, I said to myself. *In theory.*

Ah, yes—famous last words.

I readied the *Jules Verne-0* for my departure, putting

all its systems in sleep mode to conserve what was left of its power supply.

I hit the air-lock button, and the hatch quickly rose out of sight. I stepped inside the cramped air lock, hit the button on the inside, and the hatch closed again.

Then I hit the green button on the wall above me, and water started flooding the compartment. When it was full, the outer hatch rose, and I stepped out into open water—and total darkness.

I flicked the switch on my diving helmet, and my headlight flashed on—it lit a cone of terrain about six feet ahead of me and three feet wide. Everything else was out of my view.

I checked my air supply. I had exactly one and a half hours to accomplish everything I needed to do. After that the only air I had would be the supply inside the prototype.

I swallowed hard and stepped forward. My titanium boots sank deep into the black sludge on the sea bottom, sending up clouds of gray goo that blurred what little vision I had.

First, I placed most of what I was carrying with me— the extra oxygen tank, the detonator, the underwater

blowtorch, and the fuse with my watch attached—
on the metal ledge on the prototype's side.

I would have to come back for it all once I'd fastened the cable to the *Verne-1*, because there was no
way I could carry everything over there in one trip,
and the cable besides.

I climbed to the prow of the *Verne-0* and detached
the steel cable. Bud and Yo had obviously understood at least some of my instructions—they'd
played the cable out loose enough so that I could
drag it along with me across the sea bottom to the
Verne-1.

It was heavy, but down here, so was *everything*. I'd
just have to go slowly, catching my breath every few
steps along the way.

I knew the general direction of the *Verne-1*, but I
could not see it now. Nor could I swim straight to it.
My suit, covered with diving weights, was much too
heavy.

I had to watch my step, too. Scattered amid the
gooey slime were sharp-edged lava rocks. That
meant there was a deep ocean vent or fissure nearby.

I'd already known that—it was the reason the
Verne-1 had chosen this location to place its first

seismic sensor—but that didn't change the fact that this was a dangerous neighborhood.

The current was surprisingly strong, and it kept pushing the upper half of my body to the left, while my heavier lower half, weights and boots and all, stayed in place. It was a weird feeling, moving kind of like a crab across the ocean floor.

Time moved so slowly, it began to drive me up the wall. Surely, my air supply would run out before I could accomplish my mission and get safely back inside the prototype.

It was probably just my imagination, but it felt like my hour and a half was almost up. I checked my air supply again—only five minutes worth was gone. *Whew.*

At the edge of the cone of light projected by the lamp on my helmet, the mound of volcanic rubble came into view. It rose at a sharp angle—indicating that part of the *Verne-1* was buried underneath it.

Just to make sure, I maneuvered my way around the edge of the mound, until I saw the glow of light from the ship's porthole.

I was about to step toward it, when the sea floor beneath my feet gave way. I had disturbed some small, loose rocks at the edge of the mound, and they had tumbled—where?

I looked forward and down, and saw that I was standing on the edge of an even deeper trench in the sea bottom. If I took one more step, I'd sink down into the blackness for—who knew—maybe thousands of feet!

Verne-1 was trapped on a rocky ledge overlooking that trench. If I blew her stern free of the rubble and boulders, she might snap the cable, topple into it, and be lost forever.

On the other hand, if I didn't, the crew, including my dad, would all die down here. Doing nothing was not an option.

I had to get a quick look inside that porthole! How else would I ever know if my dad and the others were still alive?

In order to get there, though, I'd have to climb partway up the rubble pile, then inch forward along the top of the submersible and peek down through the porthole from above.

More time wasted—but again, what choice did I have?

I maneuvered myself slowly up the mound, taking

great care not to get stuck on anything sharp—
anything that might somehow puncture my suit's
impermeable seal and get me killed instantly.

I reached the porthole and dangled my helmeted
head down so I could see inside. . . .

10

Undersea Reunion

And there was my dad, waving to me!

You can't imagine how happy it made me to see that goofy grin on his face. Behind him, the two scientists he'd taken with him were waving too. They sure looked thrilled to see me, I'll tell you.

My dad made the talk motion with his hand, and I understood he wanted to talk to me. I made the phone sign, holding my hand to my ear with the thumb and pinky stuck out. He shook his head no, and pointed to the ship's communications console.

I understood what he meant—their radio communications were out. I could believe it. The antenna had been mounted on the stern of the ship. It must have been crushed under the weight of the avalanche.

I motioned for him to wait, then fished inside my suit's external storage compartment, and came out with a handy-dandy little item I'd been smart enough to bring along with me—a portable wireless antenna.

I fastened it to the hull of the *Verne-1*, rebooted my suit's communication device, directing it through the wireless router, and bingo! Dad and I were exchanging hellos.

So far, so good, I thought.

The words "too easy" never crossed my mind.

"Everybody in there okay?" I asked him.

"Just a few cuts and bruises," he said. "Boy, are we glad to see you! How did you get down here?"

I told him about flying the prototype out to the *Nestor*. I left out the part about Mom and Sandy.

"Good thinking, son," he said. "But I hope you've got a plan. We haven't got much power left, and our air supply is running low. We've only got about two and a half hours left."

"I detached the *Nestor's* steel cable from the *Verne-0*, and I'm going to connect it to *Verne-1*," I explained. "Then I'll follow you guys up to the surface."

"Sounds good. But can the cable pull us free?"

Uh, no. Not without an explosion.

"I've got a way to free the ship, Dad," I said. "Just give me some time."

"I'd give it to you if we had it," he said grimly. "Hurry, son. Every minute counts."

Duh. Like I didn't know that. Sometimes he treats me like I'm five years old.

First things first—I had to attach the cable to the *Verne-1*. Trouble was, the storm on the surface must have been pushing the *Nestor* around something fierce, because the cable was quickly losing its slack.

The closer I crept to the prow of the *Verne-1*, where the eye-hole was set for attaching the hook, the less free cable I had to work with. I needed to signal the *Nestor* to sail southwest—only about thirty feet or so, but it was a crucial thirty feet.

Of course, the only way to contact the *Nestor* was by the wireless connection inside the prototype!

I had to go back there anyway to get the explosive charge. I could take the extra time to re-enter the *Verne-0*—but what would happen to the loose cable in the meantime? I might lose it altogether!

No, I couldn't risk that. . . .

My eyes fell on a natural crevice at the edge of the

rock cliff. I jammed the hook into it. There—that would keep the *Nestor* from drifting any farther away.

I made my way back to the prototype, grabbed the underwater blowtorch and my improvised explosive device, and then returned to the *Verne-1*. It took about twenty minutes in all—twenty precious minutes—leaving me only about an hour for the rest of my work.

I rigged the device, jamming it under the boulders that covered the stern section of the *Verne-1*. Then I went back to the cable. I detached the hook, brought it over to the submersible's prow, and attached it properly.

There. Now everything was ready for the big bang. I laid out the fuse, as far as I could stretch it. It left me only fifty feet or so from my explosive charge—not exactly a safe distance, but there was no other way.

It was time to break the news.

"Um, Dad?"

"Yes, son? Got the cable attached?"

"Sure do."

"Great. Are you sure the *Nestor* will be able to pull us free?"

"Uh, well, first I've gotta free the *Verne-1* from the rubble," I told him.

"How on Earth are you going to do that?" he asked.

"Brace yourselves," I said. "I'm setting off an explosive charge."

"You're WHAT?!"

"I said BRACE YOURSELVES!" I shouted.

Not waiting for a reply, I fired up the underwater blowtorch and held it up to the fuse until it was lit. Then I turned and started slogging away as hard as I could.

I hit the control on the console mounted on my chest—the one I'd moved off the diving suit's left glove after the shark-tank test—to send the suit's servos into overdrive. That sped up my movements, buying me ten or twenty extra feet of distance between me and the explosion.

It was a good thing, too—because the force of the blast knocked me down so hard I almost passed out. Ten or twenty feet closer, and I'm sure I would have been done for.

I got back to my feet as the shock waves died out and tried to get a sense of where I was. My searchlight was pretty useless—the water was now as cloudy as could be—but my sense of direction led me right back to the *Verne-1*.

First I checked to see that Dad and his crew were still okay. They gave me the thumbs-up sign through the porthole, and I heaved a sigh of relief.

"Tom," my dad said, "we're going to have a talk about this later."

"Sure thing," I told him. I was so glad to see he was still alive that I didn't care if he ripped into me later.

Stepping carefully, I made my way back along the rock ledge to the scene of the blast. The water was still murky here, but things had definitely changed. I could read JULES VERNE-1 clearly on the stern section now.

That was good—it meant that section was no longer buried. But where was the rear propeller? Where were the little fins at the back of the sub?

There were still two big boulders where the rest of the ship should have been.

The *Verne-1* was still just as stuck as she'd been before the blast!

Frantically, I tried shoving the two boulders out of the way. They barely budged. I kept trying for a minute or so, as my heart rate soared so high I must have come close to passing out.

This was doing no good. No good at all. I had to come up with something else to save my dad and the *Verne-1*'s crew, and fast.

But what?

You know, funny things happen when you're fifteen thousand feet underwater. Thoughts pop into your head like oxygen bubbles. At that very moment, at the edge of total panic, an idea came into my head. A wild idea, for sure—practically insane . . .

But it just might work, I thought. Besides, what other choice did I have?

"Dad?"

"How's it look back there, Tom?"

"Better . . . better. I'm, um, going to have to go back to the prototype for something. I'll be right back, okay?"

There was a second of silence before he said, "All right."

And that was all he said.

Clearly, he'd heard the fear in my voice. He didn't bother telling me to hurry.

I pushed all other thoughts out of my head and

headed straight back toward the prototype. I was desperate now. In thirty minutes or so, my air tank would be empty. I had used my spare tank for the explosive charge. Every second counted.

I was making my way forward along the rock ledge when I felt the ground shaking beneath me.

Oh, no, I thought. *Not now—please, not now!*

In an instant, the whole ocean floor came alive and started shaking wildly. *An aftershock!*

The ground beneath me shifted violently, and I tumbled over the edge of the rock cliff, past the *Verne-1*, and down, down farther into the abyss!

11

The Monster of the Deep

Down . . . down . . . down . . .

It's amazing how fast you can fall when you're underwater—not as fast as falling through air, but close. Especially when you're weighted down.

I thought, *I could keep falling till I hit the center of the Earth and get melted into jelly.*

I banged against a boulder—YOW, that hurt!— and then landed hard on another one—OOF!

I got up and looked around. Beyond the boulders was a flat abyssal plain. The aftershock must have raised the part where the *Jules Verne-1* was trapped, I realized, because it was higher up the slope. I had no idea how much higher, or how far I'd fallen. I figured maybe thirty feet, but it could have been three times that, for all I knew. It was too dark to see much of anything.

Well, looking on the bright side, at least my long tumble was over. Now, as the water began to clear, I took stock of my situation, beaming my helmet's searchlight upward.

The slope was steep but not impossible to climb. Trouble was, it was mostly rubble—pebbles and sand—that might come loose at any time, sending me straight back down to the bottom.

Around the *Verne-1*, there had at least been some sea life. Here, there was nothing at all.

Strange. I wasn't that far away from it, yet it seemed like a whole different underwater realm—totally empty of life.

Had the aftershock scared the fish into hiding? If so, then they should be starting to re-emerge around now.

Where were they . . . ?

An eerie feeling came over me. I decided it was time to quit thinking so much and start climbing instead—especially since my oxygen meter was starting to run alarmingly low.

I clambered over the boulders that had stopped

my fall. As I crested the second and larger one, I thought I saw something move behind it.

Something *big*.

Maybe I imagined it, I thought. I kept climbing, but I also kept checking behind me, to see if anything was following me. The beam of my searchlight pierced the inky blackness.

Nothing. Just boulders and endless, flat sea bottom.

Don't be ridiculous, I told myself. *What could be down this far under the surface that would be big enough, and mean enough, to take on a human being?*

I tried to laugh it off, but it wasn't happening. I kept climbing, making slow progress, losing a foot of ground for every two feet I advanced.

Once more I looked back—and a dark cloud blanketed my vision.

What the—?

Then, out of the swirling cloud, a gigantic tentacle emerged, snaking around me and tightening its grip before I even knew what was happening!

The black cloud cleared, and I found myself staring into the blank, hungry eyes of that most elusive of sea creatures—a giant squid!

The huge tentacle lifted me up with ease. Now the

beast rose from its hiding place behind the boulder and brought me toward its gaping mouth.

Was this how I was going to end my days? As dinner for a giant squid?

"I don't think so," I said. With my free arm, I hit the button on my chest-mounted console and activated my Swift Kick Shark Zapper.

Yes, I know it was a stupid idea. A zapper designed to deliver a shock to a shark's unique electromagnetic locator organ should have had no effect on something so totally different as this giant squid.

But it was worth a try. The squid's gigantic tentacle was squeezing the life out of me, pressure suit or no pressure suit.

ZZZZTTT!!!

To my total surprise, the zapper worked like a charm! The monstrous tentacle loosened, and the giant squid bolted away, leaving me alone and gasping in a cloud of its ink.

Ah, alone at last.

I stood there, waiting for the squid's cloud of ink to clear, so that I could find the cliff and climb back up.

Nothing.

Why wasn't it clearing?

In a flash of sudden horror, I understood—the cloud had cleared, but I was still standing in total darkness.

My searchlight was dead!

By gripping me so tightly, the giant squid must have ruptured one of the wires that fed power through the suit's metallic fabric to the light on the helmet!

At this point, my oxygen and my time were running seriously low. I no longer had any idea which way the cliff was, or how far from it the squid had carried me before it let go.

The submersibles—and my salvation—might as well have been a million miles away!

I reached out blindly, stumbling a few steps in every direction, hoping to find the slope. It wasn't there.

It wasn't anywhere! Frantically, I picked a random direction and started walking blindly.

Where was I? And how was I ever going to get out of this mess?

Back to Work

"Tom! Are you there? Can you read me?"

YES—my dad's voice! I'd forgotten completely about the wireless connection with the *Verne-1!*

"Dad! I fell down the ledge, and my light's out—I can't see my way back."

"Don't panic, son. I'll think of something. . . . How much oxygen do you have left?"

"I don't know . . . fifteen minutes or so."

There was silence on the other end of the line as he took in this dismal news. "Okay . . . listen to me, Tom. We're going to get you back up here, do you understand?"

"Not really . . ."

"Just LISTEN!"

There was no arguing with him. I just shut up and listened.

And what did I hear?

Something that sounded like pots and pans being banged over and over again. It was the crew of the *Verne-1* banging on the little submersible's hull as hard as they could.

Good old Dad! I might be blind as a bat down here, but I could hear the noise they were making and could tell its direction and its distance.

The sound was coming from behind me. I'd been moving steadily off in the wrong direction!

Turning around and heading back the way I came, I soon found the boulders that were my landmark and began my climb back up through the inky blackness, toward life.

I wanted to respond to my dad's questions—he was constantly asking me if I was okay, urging me on, and sounding more and more frantic when I didn't answer—but to tell you the truth, I couldn't spare the breath.

The slope was steep, and the debris it was made of

kept giving way as I struggled forward. My dive suit was functioning beautifully, but it was still awkward at this depth. With every painfully slow move I made, I was using up more and more of my scarce air supply.

But I couldn't think about that—I had to keep going. If my air ran out, I would just die, that was all—quickly and painlessly. And so would my dad . . . and the others . . .

No! Keep going. . . . Forward . . . forward . . .

Let me tell you, you get exhausted really quickly when you're exerting yourself underwater. When I finally crested the slope and saw the *Verne-1*'s lights glowing softly, it gave me hope—and somehow, I found the strength to continue.

It had taken me a grand total of ten minutes to climb the slope. That left me with all of about five minutes, maybe seven if I was lucky, to get back to the prototype and implement Plan B.

Believe me, it was taking every ounce of strength I had, just to put one foot in front of the other. And every breath I took left me with less air to reach the *Verne-0*.

In the near darkness only the rapidly dimming light of the *Verne-1*, filtering through the now-cloudy water, gave me a sense of where I was. I could only hope my sense of direction was as reliable as it always was back on the surface.

I had shut off *Verne-0*'s power before I left her, conserving it for later. Because of that, I couldn't see her down here in the darkness. *Verne-1*'s lights weren't strong enough to cast a glow that far. Still, I knew where the prototype had to be in relation to the *Verne-1*, and that's where I was headed.

Just when I thought I was going to pass out, I bumped smack into the *Verne-0*! Not a moment too soon, either.

I opened the outer door of the air lock and pressed the button that started draining the water out of it. As soon as it got down past my neck, I wrenched my helmet off and breathed in as much air as I could hold.

I was alive—but I had just barely made it. I had to sit down for a minute to recover, even though my dad and the others were running out of oxygen themselves.

As soon as I was able to move again, I tried to radio the *Nestor*. I was going to need their help pulling the *Verne-1* up, and I could only hope the worst of the storm up there was over.

"Hello, *Nestor*, do you read me?" I waited.

Nothing.

"*Nestor! Nestor!* Come in!"

Deathly silence.

"Bud! Are you there? It's me, Tom!"

Crackling. And then, "Tom! You're alive!"

I laughed out of sheer relief. "You're still kicking too, I see."

"Man, it's been rough up here. We lost our radio antenna for awhile there, and they had to bolt it back up. The computers went on the fritz too—know who fixed 'em? It was Yo."

It didn't surprise me. Yo is an unbelievable tech wrangler. She can fix just about anything computer-related—when she isn't seasick, that is.

"Everyone okay up there?"

"Sort of. Your sister's been barfing her guts up."

"And not Yo?"

"No, man. She's been so busy fixing the computer system she forgot to be sick!"

I had to laugh—but only for a second.

"Bud," I interrupted him. "We've got a bad situation down here. I've only got about half an hour to get this right, and then I'm going to need you guys to haul away on that cable and pull up the *Verne-1* as fast as you can."

"You got her freed?" he asked. I knew Captain Walters had to be leaning over his shoulder, taking it all in.

"Um, not yet. But I've got a plan."

"You've got a *plan?* Man, what've you been doing down there all this time?"

"I'll tell you later," I said. "Bud, this is the last chance any of us have of making it back up there alive."

There was a short silence as he took my words in. Then, "What do you need us to do?"

"Like I said, in exactly one half hour, I want you to haul up the cable, as fast as it'll go. Hopefully, I'll have the *Verne-1* freed by then."

"Okay, bro. You got it. Go get 'em, Tom."

"Will do," I said. "Um, Bud?"

"Yeah?"

"If I don't see you again—well, it's been great. Tell Yo for me, okay?"

"Hey, Tom, don't talk like that. You're coming back . . . aren't you?"

"I'm planning on it," I assured him. "Just . . . well, just in case, though."

"Cool."

"Okay, then. Let's roll. Over and out."

I took a moment to examine my diving suit. It sure didn't look too good. The squid's embrace, as well as my fall down the slope, had left it much the worse for wear.

The trouble was, I was going to have to trust it with my life.

To implement Plan B, I first had to link Q.U.I.P. directly to the prototype's control systems. That took me about five minutes—not bad, but in this case, every minute used was one minute lost.

"Hello there, Tom," Q.U.I.P. said as I hooked up the final wire. "Nice to be talking again."

Since I'd taken his chip out of my watch so I could use it for the explosive charge, he'd been without a voice.

"Didn't the explosives work?"

"No. We're going to try something else."

"And what would that be?"

"Q.U.I.P.—I'm going to use the prototype to free the *Verne-1*."

"Excuse me?"

"I'm going to ram this baby into those two big boulders until the *Verne-1* is free. Correction—*you're* going to do it."

While I was telling him all this, I was busy refilling my air tank with most of the *Verne-0*'s remaining supply. That would give me a full one and a half hours worth of air—enough to get the job done and, hopefully, save myself as well.

"My calculations tell me that such a collision would result in the destruction of the prototype, Tom."

"That's right, Q.U.I.P.," I said. "I won't be needing it anymore."

"Will you be going up to the surface with the *Verne-1*, then?"

"Um . . . sort of. Don't worry about me, okay? Just follow your instructions."

"Correct me if I'm wrong, Tom, but . . . it seems to me that this plan results in the end of *me*."

"Q.U.I.P.," I said, "I'm going to do my best to save you. But if the prototype's destroyed, I'll just have to reconstitute you from the program on the super-computer."

"But Tom—"

"Q.U.I.P., it's either you or my dad. And he's . . . well,

he's nonrenewable. Besides, he's my *dad*. I know you can't really understand that, but well, that's how it is."

"I see."

But I could tell he really didn't. As intelligent as Q.U.I.P. is, he's still artificial. He doesn't have emotions.

"Well," I said, "here goes nothing."

I strapped my tank and helmet back on, stepped into the air lock, and then walked out onto the sea floor. Using the dim lights of the prototype and the *Verne-1* to guide me, I got into position, as close to the *Verne-1* as I dared to go.

"Okay," I told Q.U.I.P. over our wireless connection. "Let her rip."

I watched as the prototype lifted off the sea floor, kicking up a cloud of black mud as it went into motion.

It headed straight for the two big boulders that had crushed the rear section of the *Verne-1*, and slammed into the larger of the two, full force.

WHAM!

I felt the water push me backward as shock waves from the collision washed past me.

Shaken by the impact of the sub, the huge boulder

rolled slowly over and toppled off the *Verne-1* and down the slope I'd just climbed up.

Yes! One down, one to go.

The prototype backed away, wobbling now but still under control, and pointed itself toward the second boulder.

WHAM!

The second boulder wavered, but then fell back into place.

Again, the prototype smashed itself against the huge rock—and this time, the poor little sub broke in two! But the boulder didn't move.

"Noooo!" I screamed, watching as the last of the air that had been sealed inside the *Verne-0* leaked out of the crack in its titanium hull, sending millions of bubbles rising three miles up to the surface.

The little submersible was ruined forever—but to my surprise, Q.U.I.P. and the *Verne-0* weren't finished yet. Somehow, the prototype backed up and managed one more valiant charge—and this time, miraculously, the boulder toppled over!

As the *Verne-0* split completely in two, I saw the stern of the *Verne-1* rise out of the rubble. *She was free!*

I made my way forward now and waved to my dad

through the ship's porthole. "Everything okay?" I asked him.

"So far so good," he said. Then, "Tom, why haven't you been answering my transmissions?"

"Well, I could barely breathe for a while," I said. "And after—well, I didn't want you to know what I was up to."

I could see his expression darken. "What do you mean?" he asked.

"I've . . . I've trashed the prototype," I said.

"All right," he said, nodding. "We can jettison the rest of the seismic sensors—that will give us enough space in here for you to get hauled up to the surface with us."

"Uh, that won't work, Dad."

"Oh? Why not?"

"Because the outer door of your air lock is bashed in. Even if I could get it to work, it's no longer watertight. We'd flood the ship if we opened the inner door."

"Well, then . . . how do you plan to get up to the surface without the prototype? Do you even have enough air in your tanks?"

"Just about," I said—although the truth was, it all

depended on how long it took to drag the *Verne-1* up to the surface.

Because the only way I could get up there fast enough was by hitching a ride on the outside of the submersible.

The Rising

"Dad?" I said. "Any second now, the *Nestor's* going to start hauling up the cable." I sure hoped so, anyway.

There was a short silence. Then, "You're going to hang on to the ship, aren't you."

It was a statement, not a question.

"That's right."

I heard him swallow hard. "Hold on tight, son."

"I will."

"One more thing, Tom—it's going to get dark for you out there. We're just about out of power in here. . . . So . . . I guess we'd better say good-bye right now."

I could hear his voice get tight. "I love you, son."

"Love you too, Dad," I said.

What else was there to say?

It was time to get busy. I had to find a good spot to hang on to before the *Verne-1*'s power went out and I was plunged into total darkness—and before Bud and the captain started hauling us up to the surface.

I scanned the sub as well as I could in the semi-darkness. My gaze fell on a likely spot, on top of the *Verne-1* and toward the air lock. If I positioned myself just right, I could hold the cable with my arms locked around it. I could then brace both my feet up against the jagged, broken top of the outer air-lock door.

No sooner did the idea pop into my head than the lights of the sub dimmed, flickered, and died. The other end of my wireless connection went to static.

Okay. Now I had to find the spot without using my eyes, or talking to Q.U.I.P. or Dad.

Simple. Same as "Pin the Tail on the Donkey"—except I always stunk at that game.

Totally blind, I felt around the side of the hull until I found the air-lock door. Then—slowly and carefully, so as not to damage my suit any more than it already was—I climbed up the door, finding foot and hand holds on its jagged edges.

Finally, I hauled myself up onto the top of the submersible and wrapped my arms around the thick steel cable. I was just perfecting my footholds on the top of the door when, with a sudden jerk, the cable snapped tight.

We were being hauled up!

The *Verne-1* wobbled like crazy—front to back, back to front, and side to side at the same time! It was really hard to hang on, at least until the continual rise and pull of the cable gave the *Verne-1* time to steady itself (though it was still far from a smooth ride).

Up we went. Slowly. So slowly that I started to wonder if my oxygen—or the sub's—would hold out long enough.

The waves and wind up on the surface must have been pretty strong still, because the cable, as it rose, also swayed from side to side.

Even worse, it went up in fits and starts. Every time I tried to shift my position slightly, I nearly got knocked off the cable when it gave another yank!

Then there was the weight of the water pressing down on me hard as I rose the three miles toward the surface. At the beginning, with me and the sub at fifteen thousand feet, I felt like I was shouldering a thousand-pound weight. And while the load grew lighter as we rose, it didn't feel that way to me. That's because, over time, I was getting more and more exhausted.

My dwindling supply of air didn't help any either. The more I breathed, and the deeper the breaths I took, the less air there was for the last part of my ride.

By breathing less, I might save a few last gasps for the end—and those few gasps might be the difference between life and death.

This trip up through the regions of the sea was taking *forever*—and the fact that it was pitch-dark all around me made it really scary, too. I had no idea what was out there in the blackness. Maybe another giant squid.

It was a relief when light began to filter faintly down from the surface. The fact that I saw a school of hungry-looking sharks circling up in the distance didn't even faze me. At least I could see them—and if they came any closer, I could give them a charge with my zapper.

Now that we were getting closer to our ultimate

rescue, I began to believe I was going to make it out of this alive after all. If I got really lucky, there'd be enough air in both my tank and the submersible for us all to survive.

That's when the cable gave a sudden pull. My feet weren't braced well enough for such a sharp yank, and they slid off the edge of the air-lock door. My arms slipped, too—leaving me dangling literally by my fingernails!

I scrambled to get my arms firmly back around the cable. Then I held on for all I was worth and kicked out wildly, trying to get my feet back into position. Somehow, I couldn't seem to move them much at all. They felt like they still had those heavy weights on them—even though I knew I'd gotten rid of them.

Then why did they feel like the weights were still there? Suddenly I realized what was happening—*my legs had fallen asleep!*

Sure enough, being in one, cramped position for so long had caused them to numb out. I knew what was going to happen next—pins and needles.

OW! That really hurt!

The cable was swaying more wildly now that we were approaching the surface. It rocked me back and forth, straining my arms as I dangled like a rag doll.

I wondered if I was strong enough to hold on much longer. Looking up, I saw that the circle of sharks had grown closer, forming a tight ring around me.

Uh-oh. I could feel myself getting light-headed—just as the pins and needles in my legs were starting to calm down too!

If I didn't get myself together in a hurry, I was going to end up being pulled away from the cable by a strong set of shark jaws, then dropped to the sea bottom as soon as Jaws found out he couldn't digest my diving suit.

Not a happy ending.

Must . . . stay . . . awake . . . , I told myself. *Breathe . . . slowly. . . .*

The cable was spinning wildly in circles as we rose, but it was definitely getting lighter . . . and lighter . . .

Or was it me, getting more and more light-headed as the last of my oxygen got used up?

As I struggled to stay awake, I felt something bump up against me, hard.

"Okay," I muttered, half-asleep already. "I gotta pusha buddn . . ."

Summoning my last reserves of strength, I scrambled to get back my foothold. My legs shot bolts of pain up into my brain, but I fought through it, digging the toes of my boots into the jagged rips in the door's metal skin.

Then, holding on for dear life with my right arm, I used my left to hit the zapper button.

Like magic, in an instant the circle of sharks scattered into the distance!

I did it! I thought.

"Yes, you did, Tom. I'm proud of you."

Huh?

"Mom?"

"Hello, Tom."

Was she calling me from the *Nestor's* radio? No . . . that couldn't be it. . . . I had no contact with the ship. . . .

Oh . . . of course . . . she must be here under the water with me. . . .

But what was Mom doing here, under the water?

I was losing it—I could feel the wave of sleep wash over me . . . or was it a real wave . . . ?

I closed my eyes, put my head on Mom's shoulder . . . and let the blackness come over me.

14

Survivor

When I opened my eyes, I saw my mother staring down at me, just like in my dream.

She burst into tears. They fell onto my face, wet and warm—but real!

And even though Mom was crying, she was smiling. "Oh, Tom!" she cried. "You're alive! Thank goodness!"

"I'm . . . I'm alive?"

I was actually surprised, to tell you the truth. For a minute there, I was pretty sure I was dead. As it was, I was still gasping for breath.

"Dad?" I asked, still woozy and semi-hallucinating from the lack of oxygen.

My mom pointed up to the pod where the *Nestor's*

crane had just deposited the damaged *Verne-1*. Crew-men were working frantically to open the hatch. They pried it clear, and one of them peeked inside.

"They're alive!" he shouted, and a huge cheer went up from the entire crew.

Mom gave me a big hug, which I was too weak to really return. She helped me sit up, and that helped me get my bearings back.

The ship was still rocking in the choppy seas, but it wasn't nearly as bad as the waves we'd had on the way out here. Had it really been only yesterday?

Now it was Sandy's turn to give me a hug. "Oh, Tom!" she said, "I am so jealous."

"Huh? What do you mean, jealous?"

"You got to go to the bottom of the sea, and drive the submersible, and see all kinds of weird creatures—*and* rescue Dad! Meanwhile, I was stuck here on this nightmare of a heaving ship, blowing chunks for hours!"

"Believe me, you wouldn't want to trade the past few hours with me."

"Whatever. Next time, it's my turn."

I had to smile. "Sure thing, Sandy. You got it."

Yo appeared, kneeling down beside me. "Hey, there," she said, sniffing back a tear. "We were getting kind of worried about you."

"Me? Nah, no worries," I said, grinning. "Hey, I heard you were busy the whole time, fixing *Nestor's* computers."

Now it was Yo's turn to smile. "Somebody had to do it," she said coolly.

Bud leaned over her shoulder to catch a glimpse of me as I sat there, gradually getting my breath and strength back.

"Great job, dude," I told him, reaching up a hand to high-five him. "You timed that cable lift just right. Another minute later and I'd have been dead, another minute sooner and I'd have been left behind on the sea bottom."

"You could have just swam back up in that suit of yours," Sandy said.

"No way," I said. "I couldn't have come up fast enough that way. My air would have run out too soon."

My dad was being helped out of the *Verne-1* by Captain Walters. Everybody gave him a cheer, and he waved back, smiling. "At least we got one of the seismic sensors down," he said. "Did it send out the tsunami warning?"

"It did, sir," Captain Walters said. "Apparently, there were no lives lost, and only moderate property damage on the Outer Banks of the Carolinas. Without the warning, though . . ."

"Then this was all worth it," my dad said.

That's him—his mind is always on his mission, never on the danger to himself.

I turned back to my mom. "How did I get here?" I asked. "I think . . . I think I passed out while I was still underwater."

"You did," she told me. "The crew had to send a pair of divers in to haul you out of the water and beat off those sharks."

I closed my eyes. I had come so close to death—only seconds away, at best—that I still felt shaken.

Suddenly, a tall, athletic-looking guy with long silver hair tied back in a ponytail came up to me and shook my hand. "Well, now," he said, "I finally get to thank you."

Huh? Oh, now I recognized him, by the big purple bruise on his forehead. He was the guy I'd found floating on the remains of his boat after the freak wave hit, who I'd pulled back to safety aboard the *Nestor*.

"Sure thing," I said. "Glad you made it through."

"I made it thanks to *you*," he said. "Don't think I'm going to forget that either."

This guy looked familiar, somehow. Where had I seen his face before?

"I'm Warren Leland," he said.

Then it hit me. Warren Leland's face has been on the cover of every business magazine my dad's ever brought home. He's a multibillionaire businessman who also sails his yachts in the America's Cup races and goes solo diving for treasure.

And I'd saved his life!

"I'd like to talk to you, young man, after this is all over, about that diving suit of yours. I think it might be a real moneymaker for my investors."

"Um . . . sure," I said, sounding like a real geek. "Sure thing."

Then Dad came over, and we wrapped our arms around each other. Mom and Sandy joined in too—a big, Swift family-style sandwich.

"Son, you saved our lives," he said, his chin quivering a little. "The three of us—Holly, Bruce, and I—would never have made it without you."

It's not like my dad to get emotional—but at that moment, all of us were pretty close to losing it.

The *Verne-0* and the *Verne-1* were both trashed, and only one of the seismic sensors had been deployed.

But at least that one sensor had done its job. Besides, we still had each other.

"All right, everyone," Captain Walters shouted, "let's head for shore!"

"Amen to that!" Yo said. "I've had enough of the ocean for the next ten years!"

But wouldn't you know it, Yo changed her mind. It was only three weeks later when she dropped in on me while I was in my underground lab at Swift Enterprises.

I was at my work table, tinkering with my brand-new wristwatch, complete with a reconstituted Q.U.I.P. I was just putting the finishing touches on the watch when Yo knocked on the lab door.

"Come in!" I said.

She tiptoed in and shut the door softly behind her. "I'm sorry to disturb you," she said in a loud whisper.

"You don't have to whisper, Yo," I told her. "I can take a break for a few minutes."

"Oh. Good. Is that Q.U.I.P. you're working on?"

"Uh-huh."

"Oh." She just stood there, biting her lip.

"Is there something you wanted?" I asked.

"I was just wondering. . . . I'm going to Puerto Rico for the week with my family. . . ."

"Fantastic!" I said. "Sounds like a great time."

"Yeah . . . but I was wondering . . . what's up with that diving suit of yours?"

"Huh?"

"Is that rich dude going to buy it from you?"

"Maybe. His engineers are looking over the design, and they're supposed to get back to me."

"Oh. So . . . it's not here?"

"What, the suit? Oh, yeah, it's right over there, in the corner."

"Oh! I thought, like, y'know, it might be . . ."

"No. I just sent them the designs and a sample of the material."

"Cuz I thought maybe I could, like, borrow it for the week? I want to do some diving—nothing really deep or anything, but, y'know . . . do a little treasure hunting around some of those pirate wrecks?"

I laughed. "Sure, Yo. Take it with you. Enjoy. Bring home some gold doubloons."

"You sure?"

"Totally."

She gave me a big dimpled smile, ran over to the corner, and scooped up the suit. It was dented in a hundred places, and you could still see the squid's sucker marks imprinted on the material—but it would be fine for Yo's shallow-water diving purposes.

"You're the best, Tom," she said. "I'll take good care of it."

I shook my head and smiled. I could tell she was itching to put it on and show it off to everyone in her family.

"Have a blast," I told her. "See you when you get back."

She was out the door before I realized that I wasn't even going to be here when she got back. I was heading to New York—to United Nations

Headquarters, in fact. I'm going to be testing out my latest invention—an instantaneous translator. It can handle any human language, turning it into any other as fast as you can say *bonjour*.

It's going to put a lot of translators out of business.

THE HARDY BOYS

BOYS

They've got motorcycles,
their cases are ripped from the headlines,
and they work for ATAC:
American Teens Against Crime.

CRIMINALS, BEWARE:
THE HARDY BOYS ARE
ON YOUR TRAIL!

Frank and Joe are telling all-new stories of crime,

danger, death-defying stunts, mystery, and teamwork.

Ready? Set? Fire it up!